I0819812

TABLE OF CONTENTS

To my late beloved mother, **Sylvia (Tzila) van der Velde-Duis** — whose strength, love, and unwavering faith continue to guide my steps even beyond this world.

To my father, **Benno (Benjamin Zev van der Velde**, may God bless him with many more years of health, happiness, and light.

To my children and grandchildren, the living branches of our family tree.

To my sister, brother in law and their family;
To my aunt, **Elisa Abrams van der Velde**, and her family;
To all of our ancestors — Ashkenazi and Sephardic — who endured the hardest chapters of our people's history: the flames of the *auto-da-fé*, the terror of the Inquisition, and the unspeakable devastation of the Second World War. Many survived, many did not, and all of them left a legacy of courage that flows in our veins.

And to all those who belong to our faith, who honor it, who stand beside it, or those who hold respect for G'd's Nation of Israel

Thank you for reading this work.
I wrote it with my heart, my soul, my tears, and my smiles — and with gratitude to Hashem for allowing these words to be written at all.

May Hashem send the Redeemer soon, so the world may return to true and blessed "normal.".

Published by:
Home Safe Home Books
Home Safe Home Inc.
1133 Ocean Ave
Lakewood, New Jersey 08701
United States

Phone: **917-681-5189**
Email: **homesafehome613@gmail.com**
Website: www.homesafehomeinc.com

From the Ashes of Lisbon: A Crypto-Jewish Saga of Courage and Survival

All characters, historical settings, and cultural practices depicted in this novel are based on extensive research and ancestral records. While inspired by real historical events, specific scenes, characters, and dialogues are used fictionally for narrative purposes.

ISBN: 979-8-9997650-4-8
(Softcover & Hardcover editions)

Published by:
Home Safe Home Books
An imprint of Home Safe Home Inc.
1133 Ocean Ave
Attn: Home Safe Home Inc.
Lakewood, New Jersey 08701
United States

Phone: 917-681-5189
Email: homesafehome613@gmail.com
Website: www.homesafehomeinc.com

Publisher's Logo:
(Home Safe Home Books imprint logo appears here)

Printed in the United States of America.
First Edition, 2025.

The paper used in this publication meets the minimum requirements of the American National Standard for Information Sciences — Permanence of Paper for Printed Library Materials.

CHAPTER 1 THE HIDDEN JEWS OF LISBÓN

The morning sun rose over Lisbon with the same deceptive gentleness it had always shown, soft golden rays brushing the tiled rooftops, warming the narrow streets where merchants set out baskets of figs and olives, and fishermen pushed their small boats into the harbor. To the outside world, life in Portugal appeared peaceful, structured, and God-fearing in the way the Church demanded. Bells rang from stone towers, women crossed themselves as they passed chapels, and men hurried to avoid being mistaken for those who did not attend Mass often enough. But behind shuttered windows and locked doors, in quiet kitchens where the embers of last night's fire still glowed, there lived families like the Nunez Vas, whose hearts beat to a rhythm older than Portugal itself older even than the kingdoms that had risen and fallen along the Tagus. Families who had learned to whisper instead of speak, to hide instead of display, and to pray silently instead of chanting as their ancestors once did in the open courtyards of Toledo. And it was in one of these homes, behind thick walls darkened by age and memory, that Regina Nunez Vas began her seventeenth year. Regina known only within her family as Bu, a childhood nickname that had somehow managed to follow her into womanhood moved through the kitchen that morning with the ease and grace of someone who had spent her entire life learning to take up as little space as possible. She was slender, with long, dark hair braided down her back, and hands that carried a softness no longer common among girls of her age. Those hands, capable of weaving seven tablecloths so bright and white they looked like wedding linens, were her pride, her responsibility, and her inheritance. On the wooden table near the window lay her work: a half-finished cloth stretched across a simple frame. She leaned over it, the morning light revealing delicate patterns of flowers and vines, each stitch placed with purpose. Her grandmother had once taught her that a woman's needle could tell her story in ways her voice never dared and Regina believed it. Every thread she pulled carried memory, fear, beauty, and hope in equal measure. Behind her, the sound of shuffling footsteps signaled the approach of her mother. “Bu,” her mother called softly, glancing out the window before she spoke further. “Not so close to the light. Someone passing might see you working on a Friday morning, and we cannot risk questions. The neighbors already wonder why we leave for the countryside every week.” Regina nodded and pulled the frame back into the shadowed corner. In public, the family was Catholic. They crossed themselves, attended Mass, and made sure their names were known to the parish. But every Friday afternoon, like clockwork, they left Lisbon behind. They carried baskets, tools, and blankets, and made their way to their small rural estate affectionately called “the finger”, because it pointed like a narrow strip of land toward the hills. Once there, once hidden from the city and the eyes of the Church, they breathed again. They lit candles. They prayed. They became Jews openly, if only for twenty-four hours. It was a rhythm carved into their lives with the precision of Regina’s own embroidery. Her father entered the room next, his steps slower than they once were, one hand pressed thoughtfully against his back. He had been a scribe in his youth, then a keeper of accounts, then a farmer, and now simply a tired man who carried too many secrets in his spine. His beard, streaked with silver, gave him the appearance of someone far wiser and older than the Church liked its loyal Catholics to be. “Bu,” he said, his voice warm despite its weariness, “you’ve been awake since dawn again. You must rest your eyes before we begin the journey.” “I’m almost finished with the seventh one,” she said, unable to keep the quiet pride from her voice. Her father approached the cloth, touching the edge gently, as though it were a fragile relic. “Seven tablecloths,” he murmured. “Seven blessings. Seven promises. Your hands do holy work, even if the world cannot see it.” Before Regina could answer, the sound of hurried, heavy steps echoed from the hallway. Her brother Solomon rushed in, his simple face flushed with excitement or confusion it was always hard to tell which. His brown curls sprung in every direction, and his clothes, though neatly tied, already bore the wrinkles of someone who had rolled on the floor chasing one of the farm animals earlier that morning. “Bu!” he called, his voice too loud for safety. “Bu, look! I fed the chickens all by myself!” Regina smiled at him with patient affection. “That’s wonderful, Solomon.” Her mother, behind him, shook her head and whispered, “Slowly, Solomon. Slowly. You mustn’t shout. Remember what we said.” Solomon nodded obediently but could never fully understand why silence was necessary. He knew only that when he was too loud, Mother frowned and Father closed the shutters. But innocence has always carried its own dangers, and Regina often worried that one day Solomon’s sweet, unfiltered honesty might cost them more than a moment of fear. Outside, a wagon creaked into motion. The weekly pilgrimage to the countryside was about to begin. “Bu,” her mother said again, more gently this time, “go fetch your sister.” Regina set down her embroidery and walked through the house until she reached the small room where Hanna, her younger sister, sat humming softly to herself while arranging a row of buttons on the floor. Hanna was nine years old but had the mind of a child half her age content, cheerful, easily bewildered, yet always gentle. “Hanna,” Regina said, kneeling beside her, “it’s time to go to the finger.” Hanna looked up with bright, trusting eyes. “Will you play the flute later today, Bu?” “If you’d like.” “Good,” Hanna whispered, and she placed her small hand into Regina’s without hesitation. Together they walked outside to where their father was securing baskets to the wagon. Among the animals grazing nearby were the five creatures that made up the pride of the Nunez Vas estate: a pair of goats, a patient old cow, a small donkey with a stubborn streak, and a large chestnut horse who acted as if he supervised the entire household. It was the same every week predictable, comforting, sacred. And it was this same rhythm, this same fragile balance, that was about to shatter in only a few days, when a single cruel moment in a dusty stable would set their world ablaze and force Regina Nunez Vas onto a road she had never imagined walking. But for now for this brief, precious moment the family prepared for Shabbat with the quiet dignity that had kept their faith alive through generations of fear. Regina lifted Hanna onto the wagon. Solomon climbed in after her, humming. Their parents took their usual places. And as the horse stepped forward, the wheels rolling over the dry earth, Regina looked back at the house they were leaving behind and wondered, not for the first time, how long it could still protect them. The bells of Lisbon rang in the distance. No one knew that storm clouds were gathering. No one knew that danger already had a name. No one knew that Ricardo Castelhano had been watching her. Not yet. The wagon moved slowly along the dusty road, its wheels carving familiar grooves into the earth. The journey to the finger took nearly two hours, but it was a journey Regina cherished. Here, in the sway of the wagon and the rhythm of the horse's hooves, she felt a strange mixture of fear and freedom fear because every mile away from Lisbon increased the risk of questions, and freedom because every mile toward their secret Shabbat sanctuary brought a breath of peace the Law of the land could not offer. Her mother held Hanna securely beside her, whispering gentle reassurances as the child pointed at distant birds and swirling dust clouds. Her father rode silently, lost in his thoughts, the lines on his brow deepening as they travelled farther from the city. Solomon sat with his legs dangling over the wagon's edge, watching the ground pass beneath him as if each rock and twig carried a message intended only for him. Regina sat toward the back, her fingers absently brushing the fabric pouch that contained her embroidery needles. She carried them everywhere now tiny tools of beauty in a world growing increasingly violent. Sometimes she imagined that if she stitched enough beauty into the world, maybe the darkness would not swallow them whole. As they turned onto the road leading toward the hills, the countryside opened gently before them vineyards stretched over soft slopes, olive trees clung to rocky ground, and the soft hum of insects filled the air. The finger was hidden beyond a cluster of trees, a simple farmhouse with stables and a small barn, nothing to draw suspicion. It had been in the family for generations, long before the Church decided that Jews were safer hidden than seen. They arrived just as the sun began its slow descent, bathing everything in a warm, golden haze. Solomon jumped from the wagon before it even stopped, running toward the stable as he always did, eager to greet the animals. Hanna followed, stumbling slightly but giggling when Regina steadied her. The house welcomed them like an old friend. Its wooden beams, worn smooth by years of prayer and silence, seemed to breathe as they entered. Regina inhaled deeply, smelling the familiar mixture of hay, old wood, and the faint scent of spices her father always stored in small burlap sacks. Her mother began preparing for Shabbat, opening the small box that held their hidden candlesticks simple, silver-plated ones brought long ago from Spain. Regina gathered linens and set the table with the care she would give a royal banquet, smoothing the cloth with her palms until every crease softened. The damask glowed faintly in the candlelight; a reminder of the beautiful things the world could not take from her. Solomon collected wildflowers, as was his custom, bringing them inside in a muddied handful and dropping them proudly onto the table. “For Shabbat,” he declared. “For Shabbat,” Regina echoed, arranging them in a small clay vase. Her father laid out the oil lamps. Her mother shaped the bread dough. Hanna hummed a tune she likely invented on the spot. The entire home seemed to pulse with anticipation, with the ancient rhythm of a people who had never stopped believing that rest was holy, even when forbidden. But Regina’s mind drifted, unbidden, to the stable not to the warmth of the animals or the familiar smell of hay, but to the one person who did not belong there. Ricardo Castelhano. He had eyes that always lingered too long, hands that moved with more force than necessary, and a smile that hovered somewhere between charm and threat. Regina had seen how he watched her, how he found excuses to be near her when she was carrying buckets or gathering eggs. He worked for her father because he was strong, inexpensive, and willing to do the labor an aging man could no longer do but Regina knew well enough that strength without kindness was a dangerous thing. Her mother had warned her many times: “Bu, stay at a distance. A wolf that is fed by your hand still remains a wolf.” But the world was complicated, and so were people, and Regina, despite her youth, understood more than her parents believed she did. She had seen women in the village who disappeared for weeks, then returned with hollow eyes. She had overheard whispers priests questioning women about sins they never committed, men accusing neighbors of heresy over petty grudges, and families dragged from their homes in the middle of the night. The Inquisition was a shadow that moved without sound, and Ricardo was exactly the kind of man who would not hesitate to use it. And so Regina pushed him from her thoughts as she tied her apron behind her and stepped outside to fetch more water for the evening meal. The sky was turning a soft violet, the first stars flickering above the treetops. She paused at the well, letting the bucket drop with a hollow echo, and pulled it up slowly, watching the water tremble under the candle colored sky. Then she heard it footsteps, steady and purposeful, coming from the direction of the stables. Not her father's steps. Not Solomon's light shuffle. Not Hanna's skipping. These were heavier, familiar in a way that made her pulse quicken. She turned, her breath catching, and saw Ricardo Castelhano emerging from the shadows, his broad shoulders leaning against the stable door, his face half-lit, half in darkness. He should not have been there. Not on a Friday evening. Not on their land. "We don't need you tonight," she said, her voice steady despite the sudden chill in her limbs. "But I wanted to see you," he replied, pushing himself upright and taking a step forward. Regina gripped the bucket, her knuckles whitening. "My family is preparing for the evening. You shouldn't be here." Ricardo's lips curled into an unreadable smile. "I'm the one who decides where I belong, Regina." She stepped back, the hem of her skirt brushing the dry grass. And in that moment with dusk deepening around her, the candles being lit inside, and the beautiful sanctity of Shabbat moments away Regina felt for the first time that something terrible was approaching, slipping quietly into her life like a shadow seeking a place to anchor itself. What she did not yet know was that this moment, ordinary on the surface, would become the crack that tore her world apart. He moved with the ease of a man who believed he owned whatever he touched, a slow, rolling confidence that came not from nobility or learning or beauty, but from the raw, untampered certainty of someone who had never been told "no" in a way that carried consequences. Ricardo's boots sank lightly into the soil as he approached, his shadow stretching long behind him in the soft twilight, and for a fleeting instant the dying sun caught the edge of his jaw, revealing a smoothness that might have made him handsome had cruelty not etched itself so deeply into the lines around his mouth. Regina's breath tightened, not in panic but in a deep, internal bracing the same instinctive tightening of muscle and mind that she felt whenever she sensed a storm gathering over the sea, when the sky turned a deceptive lilac, beautiful enough to distract but heavy with an unspoken threat. She could feel her pulse flutter against her throat like a moth caught beneath fabric, frantic and seeking escape, but her posture remained still, refined, composed, as though the training of her mother's hand on her shoulder all her life had prepared her for this precise moment. Ricardo's eyes roamed her face with that unnerving, appraising gaze he had perfected the gaze of a man who measured not a woman's character or thoughts but the shape of her silence, the softness of her vulnerability, the hesitation he believed he could exploit. He closed the remaining distance between them, close enough that she could see the flecks of lighter brown near the pupils of his eyes, close enough that she felt the faint warmth of his breath, tinged with the smell of hay and something acrid beneath it. "You shouldn't fetch water alone at dusk," he murmured, his tone attempting to imitate concern but landing instead in a register that made her skin prickle. "A girl like you could meet the wrong man." His smile deepened. "Or the right one." Regina felt her fingers tighten around the wooden handle of the bucket, grounding herself in the solid, familiar texture of it, as if the grain of the wood could anchor her against the strange, disorienting way the shadows lengthened around them. She spoke carefully, choosing her words with the precision of someone who walked a tightrope. "I am not alone. My family is just inside." "Inside," he echoed, tilting his head slightly as if listening to the faint sounds of her mother preparing the candles, her father humming under his breath,

Solomon laughing softly at some small joy. “Yes… but not here.” The space between them felt suddenly constricted, too narrow for air to move freely. Regina took a small step backward not enough to reveal fear, but enough to reestablish the borders of dignity that Ricardo continuously tested. “I need to return,” she said quietly. “The light is fading.” “Let it fade,” he said, taking another step, his boots pressing into the dying grass. “You look different in the dark.” Her pulse quickened, not because she feared weakness in herself, but because she knew the landscape of men like him. She had seen it in the market squares, in the way certain men leaned too close to washerwomen, in the stories whispered by women who kept their voices low as if the mere memory of male arrogance required muted tones. Regina lifted her chin a fraction a small, instinctive act of defiance that she realized too late he recognized as such. His smile widened, a predator’s recognition of resistance. “There it is,” he whispered. “The fire. You hide it well, Regina. But I see it.” She tried to step past him, but he moved in the same breath, blocking her path with a casual shift of his body, as though her escape was a game he had already planned several moves ahead. “Why do you run from me?” he asked, his voice lowering, deepening. “Do you think yourself too pure to be noticed? Too holy to be touched?” Regina felt heat rise in her cheeks not the blush of embarrassment, but the boiling warmth of anger struggling against the constraints of safety. “I do not run,” she said, her voice trembling only slightly, “but I choose where I walk.” The words, though gentle, struck something sharp in him. His expression flickered irritation, surprise, a flash of masculine offense and he stepped closer, invading the last sliver of space left between them until she could feel the rough fabric of his sleeve brush against her arm. “You choose too much,” he said softly. “A servant girl shouldn’t speak like a queen.” Regina’s breath caught, and for a second, she feared the trembling in her chest might betray her but before he could lean closer, before he could push his advantage further, a distant voice broke through the tension like a cracking whip. “Regina!” Her father’s call, firm and steady as the tolling of a bell. The spell broke. Ricardo stepped back, just enough to slip back into the shadows with a half-smirk curling his lip, as if retreating were his choice, not hers. Regina seized the moment, lifting her skirts and moving quickly toward the house, her breath shallow but her stride unbroken. She did not look back, though she felt with the unerring instinct of a hunted animal that his eyes followed her every step. He didn't call after her. He didn't touch her. He simply watched. And sometimes, she knew, watching was far more dangerous. Regina crossed the yard with quick, measured steps, each one placed with the grace of someone who had grown up learning to move quietly, to disappear into shadows, to live lightly upon the earth so as not to draw attention. Yet tonight there was nothing light about her movement; it carried the weight of a young woman who had just seen the edge of danger and walked back from it without understanding how close she had come. The air felt different now thicker, almost humid as if dusk itself had absorbed the tension between her and Ricardo and was now holding it suspended above the farm like a dark omen waiting for its moment to descend. She did not dare look back toward the stables, where she knew he still lingered, his figure swallowed by the half-dark, but she felt him there, a presence heavy as storm clouds, his eyes marking her retreat with a possessiveness that sent a tremor down her spine. Inside the house, the familiar sounds of Shabbat enveloped her like a protective cloak. The squeak of the wooden table as her father leaned across it, adjusting the oil lamps. The rhythmic thump of her mother shaping the final loaf. The soft, contented murmuring of Hanna humming some half-forgotten lullaby as she traced circles in the dust with her fingers. And Solomon dear, innocent Solomon was singing a melody entirely of his own invention, occasionally pausing to giggle at something only he could see or understand. The moment Regina stepped through the doorway, her mother looked up, and though she did not speak a word, her eyes told a story: she saw the stiffness in Regina's shoulders, the unnatural flush on her cheeks, the forced brightness in her smile. She did not ask immediately, because Shabbat was beginning, and their home had survived countless dangers by respecting the fragile order of silence before questions. Her father motioned for her to take her place beside Hanna, and she did, smoothing her dress with a steady breath. The mother began reciting the blessing over the candles, her voice deep and solemn, baroegh atta Ado.. the kind of voice that could quiet storms or soothe frightened children. Regina closed her eyes as the ancient words filled the room, letting the glow of the flames press gently against her closed eyelids like warm hands offering comfort. She breathed in the mingled scent of spices, bread, and wax a blend so intimately tied to every memory of safety she had ever known and tried, for just a moment, to forget the way Ricardo's shadow had stretched across her path. But safety, she realized, was no longer a simple thing; it was something delicate and easily disturbed, like embroidery threads stretching too tightly across a frame. She felt her mother's hand brush lightly against hers under the table, a silent reassurance, a gesture that said: You are home now. You are safe. Regina gave the slightest nod, though deep inside she felt a subtle crack growing in the foundation of her world a shift so small that no one else yet saw it, but real enough that she sensed the beginning of something that would not be easily undone. As the meal unfolded, the family moved in their rhythmic, time-honored dance. Her father spoke softly about the week's Torah portion, Tanach, halacha, about the goats behaving stubbornly but producing richer milk, about a new patch of soil that might accept barley in the coming season. Solomon interrupted frequently with bursts of excitement, sharing stories that were sometimes true and sometimes invented, but always delivered with such earnestness that no one had the heart to correct him. Hanna rested her head against Regina's shoulder, her small fingers playing with the edge of Regina's sleeve, seeking the quiet comfort she always found in her sister's presence. Regina responded with gentle touches, smoothing Hanna's curls and whispering small reassurances into her ear. Yet beneath the surface of this peaceful tableau, Regina's thoughts churned with uneasy energy. Every detail of the encounter replayed itself with unwanted clarity: the warmth of Ricardo's breath, the intention in his eyes, the smug self-satisfaction in his half-smile, the unspoken threats hovering behind his words. She wondered what he would do next, whether he would return before they left for Lisbon, whether he would try to speak with her again, whether he would tell someone or worse, twist something in a way that would bring danger crashing down upon them all. Her mother saw it the faraway distance in Regina's gaze, the occasional stiffness when someone bumped into her elbow and after the blessing after the meal, she took Regina aside beneath the low wooden beams of the back room. The soft golden light from the candles flickered across her mother's face, revealing the network of fine lines etched there by years of fear, resilience, and fierce love. "Bu," her mother whispered, the nickname falling from her lips like a thread from a tapestry, "tell me." Regina hesitated with only a heartbeat before the words spilled out, not quickly or sharply, but in long, trembling breaths that matched the rise and fall of her chest. She told her mother everything Ricardo appearing from the shadows, the false charm dripping from his voice, the deliberate way he blocked her path, the insinuation in his words, the predatory calm with which he watched her. She did not exaggerate, but neither did she soften anything; she spoke with the precision of a woman who understood that truth was its own armor. Her mother listened without interrupting, without gasping or crying, without wringing her hands as many women would have done. Instead, she absorbed each detail the way only a mother trained by fear could: quietly, intensely, storing it like a seed of warning in the deepest part of her heart. When Regina finished, her mother placed both hands on her shoulders and looked into her eyes with a steadiness that made Regina's throat tighten. "You did right to come inside," she said in a low, even voice, "and you did right to push him away. But listen to me now Ricardo is not only a danger because he is a man without discipline. He is dangerous because he is a man without boundaries, active in the church, and people say: very close to the priest! and such men are easily swayed by pride, envy, or revenge. We will not be alone with him again, not even for a moment." A faint tremor of fear ran through Regina, but her mother's touch strengthened her. "Do you understand?" the older woman asked. Regina nodded. "Yes." "We will not speak of this to your father tonight," her mother continued. "He would confront the boy, and that confrontation would be the spark Ricardo needs to do something unforgivable. We cannot afford that." Another nod but slower this time, heavier, because Regina understood perfectly what her mother meant. Men like Ricardo thrived on accusation and martyrdom; if her father confronted him, Ricardo would twist the story, paint himself the victim, and let the Inquisition do the rest. Her mother squeezed her shoulders gently. "We will be cautious. We will be silent. And we will be smarter than him." Regina swallowed, her pulse emboldened by the fierce determination she saw in her mother's face. "I'm not afraid of him," she whispered and it was partly true. What frightened her was not Ricardo alone, but what a single lie or accusation could do in a world where Jews walked under constant suspicion, where even innocence could be construed as guilt if whispered into the right ear. Her mother brushed a strand of hair from Regina's cheek and pressed a soft kiss to her forehead. "I know, Bu. I know. But fear is not the enemy. Fear keeps us alive. Recklessness kills. Remember that." The words lingered between them, heavy and honest, reverberating with the quiet weight of a truth passed from one generation of hidden Jews to the next. As they rejoined the family, Regina felt the house shift around her not physically, but emotionally, spiritually as though the walls themselves understood that something had breached the delicate sanctuary of their lives. The candles flickered faintly as the night deepened, casting long shadows across the white damask tablecloth she had woven with such devotion. The shadows stretched and twisted with the movements of the flames, reminding her of the encroaching danger that had stepped so close to her under the darkening sky. And though she sat between her siblings, with the warmth of her father's voice filling the room, she could not escape the quiet echo that pulsed at the back of her mind a warning that curled like smoke beneath the rafters: This man will not stop. He will return. And when he does, nothing in her life will remain the same. The rest of the evening unfolded with the slow, careful grace of a family who knew that peace was a fragile visitor, one who must be cherished when present and missed when gone. Regina moved through the familiar rituals with deliberate composure, lighting lamps, folding clothes, refilling cups for Hanna when her little hands struggled with the jug, helping Solomon tie a knot in the corner of his blanket the way he liked it before lying down. Yet behind each gentle gesture, her thoughts pulsed like a quiet drumbeat, reminding her that something had shifted permanently outside those wooden walls. Shabbat was their sanctuary, but sanctuaries were only as strong as those who honored them, and tonight she felt, with an instinct sharpened by fear, that someone uninvited had pressed his gaze upon the edges of their light. Her father recited passages from memory, his voice drifting across the room with the warmth of a hearth, the cadence steady enough to soothe even the most troubled heart. Regina watched the way his eyes softened as he looked at his children Solomon with his unfiltered joy, Hanna curled at Regina's side, her breath warm and even and she felt an ache settle in her chest. What would he do if he knew? If he knew how close danger had already crept into their small refuge? If he knew that outside the glow of the candles, a young man with a twisted sense of entitlement had begun to imagine himself as judge, as owner, as conqueror? Her father was a gentle man. A wise man. A man who had already endured too many losses, too many betrayals, too many nights spent listening for footsteps in the street. He would protect them with his life but protection sometimes demanded knowledge, and knowledge demanded action, and action demanded consequences the family might not survive. Her mother was right: to tell him now would be to strike a match in a room filled with lamp oil. So Regina kept silent, even when her father touched her hand at the meal's end and asked softly if she was well. She nodded, because nodding was easier than speaking, and speaking would have opened a door she did not yet have the courage to walk through. He did not push her he never pushed any of them but she saw the faint shadow of concern settle into the corners of his eyes, and she wished she could lift it with truth instead of silence. Night deepened around them, the countryside settled into the slow, rhythmic breathing of crickets and rustling leaves. Outside, the sky had turned a deep indigo, heavy with the scent of summer grass still warm from the sun. The candles began to burn low, their f lames flickering like small hearts resisting sleep. Hanna curled into her lap, her head warm and heavy against Regina's thigh, while Solomon sat cross-legged on the floor humming a tune whose logic only he understood. Her mother washed the last of the dishes, her movements graceful and practiced, each gesture carrying the weight of centuries of hidden Jewish womanhood: quiet mastery, quiet fear, quiet endurance. When her mother finally joined her father on the woven mats spread across the floor, Regina looked once more toward the closed door, as if drawn to it by an invisible thread. The wood stood firm, locked, secure but for the first time in years, she felt a whisper of doubt. How much could a simple door protect? How much could a lock withstand? Would it hold against lies? Against guilt twisted into accusation. Against a young man who felt wronged by the mere existence of her refusal? She brushed the thought aside, not because she believed it unworthy, but because her body ached with exhaustion, the kind that comes not from labor but from carrying fear like a stone beneath the ribs. When she finally lay down beside Hanna and pulled a blanket over them both, her mind lingered on the edge of wakefulness for a long time, replaying the scene by the well not just the words, not just the closeness, but the underlying message: You do not decide. I decided. That notion that arrogance unsettled her more deeply than the touch of his hand or the tone of his voice. It was the thought of being stripped of choice, of being defined by someone else's desire, of being cornered into a future not of her making. A Jewish girl in Portugal already carried the weight of laws designed to crush her spirit, but now she sensed a new weight, heavier because it was personal, because it knew her name. Eventually, her eyes drifted closed, though lightly, like a bird settling onto a branch but ready to fly at the slightest tremor. The sounds of her family sleeping filled the small home her father's gentle breathing, her mother's soft sighs, Hanna's tiny murmurs and for a moment Regina let the warmth of their presence soothe the last frayed threads of her spirit. But in the darkness, in that fragile hour between vigilance and sleep, somewhere outside near the stables, a horse shifted restlessly, stamping the ground twice as if sensing the disturbance in the air. And Regina, though she did not hear it, shivered beneath her blanket, the faint echo of that distant hoofbeat rippling through her dreams like a warning she could not yet understand. Hours later, when dawn crept timidly across the horizon, brushing pale light over the farm and touching the tops of the olive trees with silver, Regina awoke with the strange certainty that something had been set into motion something unstoppable, something that would alter the path of her life in ways she could not yet imagine. She rose quietly, stepping outside into the early morning chill, wrapping her shawl around her shoulders as she breathed in the scent of dew and earth. The world looked unchanged peaceful, tender, untouched but beneath its surface lay a tension alive and humming. And when she looked toward the stable, toward the place where Ricardo had stood the night before, she felt a tightness in her chest, as though an invisible hand were gently but insistently pressing against her ribs. This day, she knew, would lead her closer to the moment that would shatter everything. But she did not yet know how quickly fate approached. Nor how violently it would arrive. The morning unfolded slowly, with that deceptive softness that comes before a storm, the kind of morning that seems almost determined to lull its inhabitants into believing that the world is gentler than it truly is. A thin veil of mist curled among the trees, drifting lazily across the ground as the sun rose, painting the horizon in fragile hues of rose and gold. To anyone passing through, the Nunez Vas farm would have appeared serene a modest sanctuary nestled between the hills, its whitewashed walls catching the first rays of daylight, its animals stirring peacefully in their pens as though unaware of the danger's men carried in their hearts. Regina stepped outside, her shawl wrapped tightly around her shoulders and breathed in the cool morning air. The scent of damp earth and hay filled her lungs, grounding her briefly in a moment of calm. She paused, letting her eyes travel across the familiar landscape the old olive tree her father pruned every spring, the chicken coop Solomon loved to fuss over, the narrow path leading toward the vineyard where her mother collected herbs on warm afternoons. All of it felt immeasurably precious today, as if her senses had sharpened overnight, heightening her awareness of every comforting detail, every glint of dew on the grass, every distant birdsong. Yet beneath that heightened awareness lay an unspoken tension, a tightening of instinct, an alertness that pulsed quietly beneath her skin. She could not explain it in words only that something in the air felt unsettled, as though the earth itself had shifted slightly underfoot. The peacefulness of the morning felt like a fragile veil stretched too thin, one that could tear with the slightest pressure. She listened for sounds not consciously at first, but with the awareness of someone who had already seen danger in the eyes of a man who felt entitled to her fear. The usual noises greeted her: the soft cooing of doves near the roof, the groan of a wooden gate swinging gently in the breeze, the distant rustle of Solomon attempting to coax the goat away from chewing his sleeve. All of it was familiar, reassuring. And yet, Regina remained still for a moment longer, her gaze sweeping across the yard, drawn toward the stables without willing it. The stable doors were closed, the wood still dark with night's moisture, and at first glance nothing seemed amiss. But the memory of Ricardo standing there the evening before leaning against the post as though the world belonged to him, his eyes appraising her with confidence that had no place on this sacred land rose in her mind with unwelcome clarity. She felt again the echo of his nearness, the subtle menace threaded through his voice, the arrogance with which he presumed access to her life. Her hand tightened reflexively on the edge of her shawl. She stepped back inside the house, forcing herself to breathe evenly, not wanting her family to sense the unease that lingered within her. Her mother stood by the hearth looking at the soup for the shabath, so was rotating her arms to break the stiffness, from the tens situation, her movements slow and rhythmic. Solomon attempted to help by setting out bowls though one slipped from his hands and rolled across the floor before Regina caught it with a deftness that made him clap in delight. Hanna sat at the table humming nonsense tunes, tracing little circles on the wood with her fingertip. "Did you sleep, Bu?" her mother asked without turning her head, her voice steady but curious in that way only a mother's intuition can be gentle, probing, aware. "Yes," Regina answered softly. "Enough." Her mother paused only a heartbeat before nodding; she did not press further. Regina was grateful for it. Some truths were easier to face in silence. As they settled into the morning meal, her father joined them, rubbing the sleep from his eyes with the weariness of a man who carried the burdens of two lives the one he lived publicly under the watchful gaze of the Church, and the one he lived privately, hidden beneath tradition and faith. He smiled at his daughters, at Solomon's crooked attempt to fold a napkin, at his wife's careful steering the chamin (sefardic chullent) kept warm under the blankets, and for a moment everything felt normal again, as though the world had not shifted in the night. But even as Regina tried to settle into the comforting rhythm of breakfast, her thoughts drifted then tugged then pulled inexorably back toward the stables. Once the meal was finished and her father moved to feed the animals, Regina rose, intending to fetch water for washing and then begin helping to lay the table. Hanna tugged her hand, asking if she could help scatter grains for the chickens, and Regina nodded, ready to oblige. Yet as they stepped outside and Hanna scampered ahead, Regina felt it again that tightening, that instinctual prickle that made her breath catch. Her gaze drifted, first to the stables, then to the surrounding trees, then to the shadows still clinging to the edges of the yard. Nothing moved. Nothing stirred. And yet the feeling persisted, like the low rumble of distant thunder just beyond the hills. She guided Hanna toward the chicken coop, handing her a small pouch of grain, watching her scatter it with childlike enthusiasm while Solomon followed behind, humming to the chickens as though they understood his every word. Regina laughed softly at the sight it was impossible not to but the sound carried an undertone of tension she could not hide from herself. The goats bleated from across the yard, eager for attention, and her father's voice drifted toward them as he attended to the old cow. Everything seemed in its rightful place. Until it wasn't. From the corner of her eye, she noticed something small, almost imperceptible shift in the sliver of shadow near the stable door. It might have been the breeze. It might have been her imagination. But Regina felt it like a pull inside her chest, urging her to look more closely. She stepped forward, leaving Hanna with Solomon, and approached slowly, her heartbeat accelerating with each step. The stable stood quiet, the kind of quiet that does not comfort but whispers. As she drew closer, she saw it: a faint indentation in the dirt near the door, the shape unmistakably fresh a boot print, larger than her father's, pressed deep as though the person had stood there for some time. Her breath caught. She crouched, running her fingers lightly along the edge of the print. Ricardo. He had been here. Where he should not have been. When he should not have been. Watching. Waiting. A shudder passed through her, not dramatic but cold and certain. She stood slowly, glancing back toward the house, toward her mother standing in the doorway brushing crumbs of the table cloth, Regina looking for her father unaware of the danger only steps away. For a fleeting moment, she wanted to run to them, to tell them everything, to gather them inside and bolt the doors but she knew instinctively that revealing her fear too openly would not protect them. Not yet. And so she kept her silence, though her heart carried the truth like a stone. She brushed her palms on her skirt, inhaled deeply, and turned back toward Hanna and Solomon, determined to continue the morning's tasks as if nothing had changed. But she felt it. The shift. The warning. The beginning of something unavoidable. By midday, when the sun sat high in the sky and the heat softened the edges of every shadow, Regina would find herself again near the stables this time with Solomon and Ricardo, with the new stallion restless in his pen, with the air charged so heavily that even the animals sensed it. And by dusk, the world that had existed that morning would no longer be whole. Regina Nunez Vas, still unaware of the full extent of fate's cruelty, stepped back toward her siblings with a composure she no longer felt. The day stretched before her, deceptively ordinary, but the echo of the boot print near the door whispered a truth that gnawed at the edges of her calm: Something devastating was already on its way. The midday sun rose steadily, casting long, shimmering bands of light across the yard and warming the white stones beneath Regina's feet as she moved among her chores. It was the kind of heat that softened the edges of everything sounds, shadows, even thoughts wrapping the farm in a gentle haze of late morning languor. Under any other circumstances, she would have welcomed it, would have let the warmth soak into her bones while she worked with the calm, familiar movements of someone who understood the rhythm of rural life. But today the warmth only made the tightness in her chest more pronounced, the air thickening around her until it pressed against her skin like an invisible weight. Solomon followed her with the eagerness of a loyal puppy, humming to himself as he carried a small wooden crate filled with carrots he had insisted on pulling from the ground himself. The carrots were crooked and stubby, some of them barely formed, but Solomon loved them because he had grown them, and Regina never corrected his pride, only smiled and praised him as though each malformed root were a treasure. Hanna skipped ahead, her cloth doll, made by Regina with love, from remnants of material. occasionally lifting her to her nose with a delighted sigh. Every detail of the morning should have felt familiar, grounding, comforting the cluck of the hens as they searched for scattered grains, the gentle sway of the olive branches in the breeze, the steady thud of her father's boots as he moved from animal to animal, the rustle of her mother's skirts as she walked up and down the lawn, and yet Regina felt suspended, as though the entire farm were balancing on the cusp of something unnamed and enormous. The quiet was too quiet. The sunlight too bright. The peace too complete. Sometimes, she had learned, peace was not a gift. Peace was an omen. She told herself she was imagining things. Fear could distort reality, stretching a shadow into a monster, turning an ordinary silence into a threat. But when she walked past the stable again, carrying the bucket she had filled at the well, her eyes were drawn once more to the faint disturbance in the soil by the door a second

print now, the outline slightly blurred as though the morning breeze had brushed the surface. It was not her father's. It was not Solomon's. It was not any hired helper's. Ricardo had come back. He had likely stood there watching them watching her at dawn, hidden in the fog while the rest of her family stirred sleepily inside. The thought settled deep into the center of her chest, heavy and cold. Men like Ricardo rarely felt shame when they crossed boundaries; they felt entitlement. And men who felt entitled grew bold when unchallenged. She straightened slowly, letting her breath fill her lungs in a steadying wave, and turned deliberately away from the stable, unwilling to give fear the satisfaction of controlling her steps. Solomon tugged her sleeve. "Bu," he said, his voice excited and bright, "the new stallion wants to see me. I heard him. He was talking." Regina smiled faintly, brushing her fingers through his curls. "Valentino doesn't talk, Solomon. He snorts." "He talks," Solomon insisted. "He said my name. And he's lonely." Hanna giggled. "Maybe he wants a carrot." Solomon gasped as though she had revealed a profound secret. "Yes! Yes, he loves carrots! I will bring him two." Before Regina could stop him, Solomon began lumbering toward the stable with the wide, uncertain gait of a child who did not perceive danger until it stood directly before him. Regina followed quickly, Hanna in tow, trying to keep her pace calm so as not to alarm either of them. She did not want to forbid Solomon from visiting Valentino; the stallion was beautiful, powerful, and newly bonded to the family and Solomon, in his gentle way, had a gift with animals that often amazed even their father. But today, something inside her whispered caution. When they reached the stable, Regina placed a steadying hand on Solomon's arm. "Wait, let me look inside first." Solomon blinked up at her with wide eyes. "Why? Valentino likes me." "I know he does. But let me go first." Hanna peered into the shadows beside Regina, clutching her dolly as though she might protect her. The interior of the stable was dim compared to the brightness outside, the thick wooden beams cutting the sunlight into slender strips that lay across the straw covered floor like broken paths. Dust motes drifted through the air, dancing lazily in the beams of light. Valentino stood in the far stall, his sleek chestnut coat gleaming even in the subdued light, his large dark eyes following their movement with quiet curiosity. Everything looked normal. Peaceful. Ordinary. And yet Regina felt something unsettled just beneath the surface of the moment a subtle dissonance, like a musical note slightly off pitch. She listened closely, but there was no rustling, no footsteps, no human presence hidden in the shadows. No sign of Ricardo. Not yet. She stepped inside, letting her eyes adjust fully to the dimness, and placed a hand on Valentino's muzzle. The stallion exhaled warm air against her palm, then nudged her shoulder with an affectionate insistence that made her smile despite the tension tightening her spine. "See?" Solomon said triumphantly, thrusting the carrots toward her. "He wants these." "You may give him one," Regina said gently, "but stand beside me." Solomon obeyed immediately, his trust in her absolute. Hanna lingered just behind them, humming softly as Valentino chewed the carrot from Solomon's outstretched hand. For a moment, it was peaceful. For a moment, Regina allowed herself to breathe. For a moment, she believed perhaps foolishly, but earnestly

that the fear coiled inside her might unwind itself. But then she heard it. A sound so faint that she almost convinced herself she had imagined it

a quiet shift of weight, the almost imperceptible scrape of a boot against wood, coming from the shadows behind the outer stall wall. Regina's breath froze. Solomon, oblivious, reached for his second carrot. Hanna hummed louder. Valentino flicked his ears, his body stiffening. Regina turned her head slightly, her eyes narrowing as they searched the dimmest corner of the stable. Nothing moved. But the scent in the air had changed faintly, sharply the way it changes when a man is nearby, sweat and leather and something sour beneath it. She did not move. She did not speak. She only placed a guiding hand on each sibling, her voice steady and low. “We’re going back to the house now.” Solomon frowned. “But Valentino “Valentino will be here later.” Hanna tugged her skirts. “Bu, why are you scared?” “I’m not scared,” Regina said and she willed it to be true “I just want to help Mama.” But her heart beat faster now, a steady trembling beneath her ribs that no lie could soften. She guided the children out into the sunlight, glancing once over her shoulder. The stable remained still. Silent. Empty. But Regina knew with the same certainty she felt the day Hanna was born, with the same instinct she trusted when Solomon wandered too far toward the orchard that someone had been there. Someone had been listening. Someone had been watching. The moment they stepped outside, Valentino let out a sharp, sudden whinny not of fear, but of agitation and stamped his hoof hard, the echo reverberating across the yard like a warning. Regina tightened her grip on Solomon’s small hand. Something was coming. Something already set in motion. Something that would break open before the sun reached the treetops. And when it came, she would not be ready. No one would. The rest of the afternoon unfolded under a sky too blue, too clear, too deceptively serene to belong to a world carrying danger in its folds. The sun hung high above the Nunez Vas home, its light scattering over the dusty path and glinting off the metal pail by the well, painting everything in the golden glow that usually made Regina feel safe. But today, the brightness only sharpened things every shadow too defined, every movement too noticeable. Even the air seemed stretched thin, buzzing faintly like a taut string pulled too hard and ready to snap. She tried to continue with the daily rhythm of life, though her mind kept circling back to that faint scrape inside the stables, the second boot print near the door, the way Valentino had stiffened, as though sensing something she couldn’t yet see. Her mother noticed her quietness, of course mothers always did but she said nothing, only gave Regina a long, searching look as she kneaded dough at the kitchen counter. “Bu,” her father called from outside, “if you have a moment, join me with the goats. They’re restless today." Restless. Yes. Everything was restless today. Regina washed her hands, tied her shawl more firmly over her shoulders, and stepped outside again, the sun now dipping slightly, warming the top of her head while a light breeze brushed against her cheeks. She found her father near the goat pen, raising the latch while murmuring softly to the animals, his voice low and calming in that way only gentle men possess. "Strange," he said. "They've been skittish all day. I wonder if a fox passed through the night." Regina opened her mouth to speak, to tell him that it wasn't foxes that walked in boot prints and leaned against stable walls, but the words stuck in her throat. She didn't want to start a fire she wasn't sure she knew how to control. Not yet. Not while she was still hoping desperately that the danger would pass on its own. Her father touched her elbow softly. "You're quiet today." "I didn't sleep well," she said simply. He studied her for a moment, then nodded, accepting her answer without pressing. He had never been the kind of father who demanded confessions. He simply made space for them. "Go help your mother," he said gently. "I'll finish here." She nodded, but as she turned away, she felt an uneasy sensation, like a cold breeze brushing the back of her neck. She glanced toward the stable. The door was partly open now just a sliver, barely noticeable, but she was certain it had been fully closed when she left it earlier. Something twisted inside her stomach. She watched it for a moment longer, her pulse tapping faster, then forced herself to return to the house. The children's laughter drifted toward her Solomon trying to imitate a rooster while Hanna shrieked with amusement and for a moment she allowed that sound to anchor her, to remind her of why she kept her fear quiet. Inside the house, her mother was placing the risen dough into the oven. The warm smell of chamin and other Shabbat foods , wrapping the room in a sense of normalcy. Regina helped prepare vegetables for the evening meal, slicing, cleaning, arranging, but her hands felt disconnected from her thoughts, moving by habit rather than intention. As the sun neared the horizon, casting the farm in long amber shadows, her mother handed her a bowl. "Bu, take this to your father before it cools." A simple task. Ordinary. Safe. Regina nodded, wiped her hands on her apron, and stepped outside once more. The air was cooling now, taking on that early-evening crispness that made the olive trees whisper in the wind. She walked toward the back of the yard where her father usually stood during this hour praying the mincha for Shabbat, humming his quiet melodies. She didn't find him there. Instead, she found the stable door hanging fully open. Not wide. Just open. An invitation. A warning. A mistake. Her breath tightened. She took one step forward, then another, her sandals pressing softly into the dust. The stable interior was darker now, the light inside tinted with the fading gold of late afternoon. Valentino shifted in his stall, tossing his head restlessly, his hooves scraping the floor in short, agitated bursts. "Papa?" she called softly. No answer. She took another step. The smell inside was different. Heavier. Human. Sweat, leather, and something metallic beneath it a scent she recognized from the night before, from the closeness at the well. Ricardo. The bowl trembled in her grip. At first, she saw nothing. Only the dim light, the restless stallion, the scattered straw on the ground. Then she saw the shadow. Not falling from a beam. Not cast by an animal. A shadow belonging to someone standing just behind the stall partition. Watching her. Her breath hitched, her heartbeat leaping to her throat. Her father was nowhere in sight. She stood frozen for a single, stretched moment that felt like an entire lifetime then the figure stepped out of the shadows. Ricardo, Smiling. As though he had been waiting all afternoon for this precise moment. "Regina," he said softly, almost tenderly. "There you are." Her hands tightened around the bowl so fiercely that the ceramic rim pressed into her skin, and Valentino let out a low, uneasy rumble from his stall. Everything in her screamed to run. But there was no one behind her. No one nearby. No one to call her name and break the spell. Just the fading sunlight outside. Just the darkness of the stable. Just Ricardo. And fate at last stepping into the open.

CHAPTER 2 RICARDO, THE FARMHAND

The Story of Regina Nunez Vas The morning mist, Sunday morning still lingered along the edges of the vineyards when Regina stepped out of the house, her skirt brushing through the low-lying shreds of fog that clung stubbornly to the stones of the courtyard. There was a fragile serenity in those early hours, a kind of hush that seemed to cradle the estate before the harsh business of daylight returned. She breathed in the scent of earth gently warming beneath a sun not yet fierce, the scent of olive groves whispering with a faint metallic shimmer as the wind threaded through their slender leaves. The small basket she carried was filled with herbs her mother needed before midday; she planned to sort them carefully, drying what must be dried, bruising what must be bruised, all for the quiet rituals that marked their hidden Sabbath each week. The estate moved slowly at this hour, almost reluctantly, as if it wished to postpone the demands placed upon it. Sheep bleated lazily near the pens; a solitary cart wheel protested somewhere in the distance as a worker adjusted its iron rim; a rooster announced the hour with such conviction that Regina couldn't help but smile at his self-importance. These simple sounds soothed her, for within them she sensed the fragile continuity of her family's survival routine, repetition, and the pretense of normalcy that guarded the truth of who they were. Yet even in that calm, Regina carried the awareness that they walked through their lives like shadows moving along a thin border: one misstep could expose them to a world eager to devour anything it did not understand. Every lowered voice, every shutter drawn too quickly, every careful glance exchanged at the sound of unfamiliar footsteps reminded her that peace in Portugal was never a promise, only an illusion. Their estate, beautiful as it was, remained as much a sanctuary as it was a cage built of secrets, fear, and the ever-present memory of the Inquisition's reach. She was crossing the path toward the herb garden a path worn smooth by years of her mother's footsteps when she noticed movement near the low stone wall that marked the boundary of the pastures. At first she thought nothing of it; one of the older workers often checked the wall for loose stones in the mornings. But as the figure straightened, brushing dust from his palms, the shape resolved unmistakably into the broad-shouldered form of Ricardo Castelhano, whose presence had become as intrusive in recent months as the weeds that insisted on creeping into her mother's herb beds. Ricardo wiped his forehead with the back of his hand, though the day had barely begun. His shirt hung open as usual, exposing a chest hardened by labor and browned by the relentless sun, an image he seemed to cultivate deliberately, as if his bare strength were a blunt weapon he wished the world to admire. The coarse hair curling across his chest and arms made him look older than he was, though Regina suspected he was not yet twenty. What unsettled her was not his appearance but the way his eyes sharpened whenever they landed on her, a look too long, too familiar, and too entitled. The moment he noticed her, that expression flickered to life, mingling hunger with a kind of resentment, as though he begrudged the world for giving her the refinement he would never possess. He leaned one arm across the top of the stone wall, positioning himself as though he were the master of the land and she the trespasser. "Well," he said, the corners of his mouth lifting into a slow, self-satisfied grin, "if it isn't our little senhora awake with the morning sun." She neither paused nor returned his smile. Her voice carried the polite distance expected of a young woman raised properly. "Good morning, Ricardo. My mother needs these herbs, so I must hurry." His expression tightened with irritation, for he did not like being dismissed. "You always walk as if you had a crown on your head," he muttered, his voice sinking into a low, contemptuous vibration. "As if you were better than the rest of us." "I never said anything of the sort." Regina attempted to step past him. "Now please move." He did not move. Instead he shifted just enough to make her pass dangerously near if she wished to continue, forcing her to choose between confrontation and submission. She could feel his gaze lingering on her, not with admiration but with a simmering bitterness that made her skin prickle. His voice dropped as he leaned closer. "You think no one sees the strange things your family does," he murmured. "The way you vanish every Sunday night, until next Friday afternoon The foods you refuse. The words you whisper that are not Portuguese." Regina's hands tightened around the basket's handle, though she willed her voice to remain steady. "We pray in Portuguese, Ricardo. And families have their ways. Nothing more." He gave a sharp laugh. "Your ways. Yes. I've seen your ways." The tone half sneer, half accusation sent a ripple of unease down her spine. She tried to walk on, but he moved with her, close enough that she felt the heat of his breath. "A girl like you," he said, voice thick and mocking, "should know how to look properly at a man. Instead of giving him that cold statue stare. It isn't respectful." Regina stopped and turned toward him then, summoning every ounce of the quiet dignity her mother had instilled in her since childhood. "Respect," she said evenly, "is earned through decency, Ricardo. Not demanded with threats." He flinched ever so slightly, surprised that she would speak so plainly, but he recovered quickly, his jaw tightening. She stepped past him, refusing to look back, but she felt his gaze burning into her shoulders long after she had returned to her chores. By midday the intensity of the encounter had dulled beneath the familiar rhythms of household work. She washed vegetables, sorted spices, helped little Hanna braid her hair into two neat plaits, and later checked on Solomon, who sat hunched over a primer scribbling clumsy letters while their father guided his hand. These moments grounded her, restoring a sense of normalcy she desperately needed. When Regina returned to the courtyard to fetch water, she noticed her mother standing at the kitchen door, arms folded, her face taut as she watched her approach. "Regina," she whispered urgently, "come here." Regina set down the bucket and crossed the few steps that separated them. Her mother's tone was neither anger nor scolding, but something colder a quiet fear concealed beneath a veneer of composure. "That boy," her mother said, keeping her voice low though no one was nearby. "Ricardo. He watches you too much. His eyes follow you in ways no mother could ignore. You must stay away from him." Regina hesitated. "Did he say something to you?" "He did not have to," her mother replied. "A woman learns to recognize the kind of man who feels the world owes him something. And when such a man is crossed, even unintentionally, he seeks to take back what he believes was denied him." "I never encouraged him," Regina murmured. "I know." Her mother touched her cheek, her hand warm but trembling slightly. "You carry yourself with modesty and care. But even that cannot shield us. You must keep your distance from him, even if it requires coldness he will not understand." Regina nodded, though a weight settled heavily in her chest. She disliked pretending rudeness, even to those who deserved none of her kindness, yet she trusted her mother's instincts more than her own. "Good," her mother said softly. "Now help me with the bread and stay away from the stables today." But life does not always bend to warnings, and fate seldom delays its catastrophes for the sake of a mother's intuition. The sun dipped low by late afternoon, laying a soft golden wash across the fields. Regina was tidying the kitchen when Solomon burst in with breathless urgency, tugging at her sleeve and pleading for her to come see the magnificent black stallion Valentino who had been neighing loudly in restless excitement. Solomon's wide, innocent eyes shone with a childlike mixture of fear and fascination. Regina knew she should refuse; she had promised. But she could no more deny Solomon than she could deny the tide its return to shore. She followed him to the stables. The air inside trembled with the mingled scents of hay, leather, and animal musk. The beams overhead caught the last amber traces of daylight, making the dust motes dance in slow motion. And there, exactly where she dreaded he would be, stood Ricardo stroking Valentino's gleaming flank with proprietorial pride. When he noticed Regina, his mouth twisted into a slow smile that suggested he believed the universe itself had delivered her into his hands. "Couldn't stay away," he murmured, stepping toward her with the lazy confidence of a man who mistook a coincidence for destiny. Regina ignored him. “Solomon wanted to see Valentino. Nothing more.” Solomon wandered toward the stall door, humming quietly as he traced the grain of the wood with his fingertips. Ricardo, however, closed the distance between them, lowering his voice to a murmur meant only for her. “That is enough,” she warned, but her voice trembled ever so slightly. He l unged at her in attempt to grab her wrist, being so close , that she could smell the stale ale on his breath. Startled, she tumbled backward into the hay stack he looking at her, from above, glowering over her, “Don’t act so pure,” he hissed. “You think your fancy family and your quiet airs make you untouchable?” Regina recoiled, the sharp hay scratching her delicate skin until she bled, he pushed her down, trying to pin her, with a swift movement, she was able to break free just long enough to escape his clutches while screaming “Jewish girls don’t do this” she screamed, acting out of instinct loosing her caution. The words hung in the air like a lit fuse. Ricardo froze, his expression contorting from shock to something far darker. “Jewish,” he

repeated slowly, his voice thickening with malice. “So I was right.” Regina felt her pulse hammering in her throat. She opened her mouth to speak she did not know what she planned to say but she was too slow. Ricardo still hovering over her, threatening the worst… Regina’s scream caught in her throat. Solomon let out a trembling whimper that echoed like a wounded bird’s cry. Driven by instinct and desperation, Regina slapped Ricardo as hard as she could. The sound cracked through the stable like a whip. For a moment he staggered, startled. Then his rage surged. He grabbed her by the shoulders and threw her back into a heap of hay with such force that her breath left her body. That was when Solomon, shaking with fear, reached behind him and unlatched Valentino’s stall door. The rest came in a blur of hooves and terror. A thunderous crack split the air as Valentino burst forward, the powerful stallion rearing with a force no man could withstand. Ricardo turned just in time to see the massive creature charge. One iron hoof struck him squarely in the spine, the sickening crack echoing through the beams. A second hoof crushed the side of his face, shattering bone with brutal finality. His scream dissolved into a wet, terrible gurgle. Regina scrambled up, chest heaving, grabbed Solomon by the hand, and fled, her legs carrying her faster than reason. Behind her the stallion reared again, silhouetted in the dying light less an animal and more an omen sent to announce the unraveling of everything she believed safe. Her mother met them at the doorway, her face draining of color as she took in Regina's disheveled hair, torn sleeve, and Solomon's trembling form. "What happened?" she demanded, voice barely controlled. Regina's words tumbled out in a whisper. "Ricardo… he he tried…" Her mother's eyes hardened, not with surprise but with terrible certainty. She pulled Regina into her arms with ferocity. "That man is a filthy beast," she muttered, her fury trembling beneath her breath. "But listen to me carefully now: you must not say a word of this to anyone. Not to the workers. Not to the priest. Not even to the medic." "What? Mama " "No," her mother insisted, gripping her face gently but with urgency. "Even the truth, when spoken by a Jew, becomes poison in the hands of those who wish us harm. They will twist your words, turn his sins into yours, and make monsters of us all. Silence is our only shield." A medic arrived soon after, and Ricardo broken, bleeding, barely conscious was carried away on a wooden cart. No questions were asked. No explanations offered. And the Nunez Vas family said nothing. That silence, born of fear and shaped by centuries of exile, would prove to be the spark that set ablaze the dreadful chain of events waiting just beyond their sight. Long after the house grew quiet, Regina lay awake in her narrow bed, staring into the shadows, feeling the tender bruise forming beneath her ribs. The night seemed too still, too heavy, as though the air itself was holding its breath. She did not yet know the magnitude of the storm that would soon crash upon them. But somewhere deep inside her, s he felt it beginning. Like smoke curling beneath a locked door.

CHAPTER 3 THE STALLION INCIDENT

For the rest of that evening the estate moved as if underwater, every sound muffled, every gesture slowed by a heaviness that none of the servants could name but all of them felt. The cart carrying Ricardo away had rattled down the lane with such finality that even the chickens fell silent for a time, and when the dust finally settled back onto the stones of the courtyard the Nunez Vas household stood suspended in a strange, brittle quiet, as though one wrong word might shatter the delicate shell of safety that still surrounded them. In the small parlor near the kitchen, where the shutters were half closed against the coming night, Regina sat on a low stool while her mother bathed the scratches on her arms with cool water scented faintly with lavender. The sting of the cloth against her bruised skin was almost a relief; it reminded her that what had happened in the stables belonged to the world of the real and not to some fevered dream. Solomon hovered near the doorway, his back pressed to the wall, fingers twisting at the edge of his tunic; he had not spoken since they ran from the stable, and his silence weighed as heavily on Regina as the memory of Valentino's pounding hooves. Her father entered quietly, his steps slow, his face older than it had looked that morning. He had gone to the stables after the medic left, had spoken to the workers who had gathered there, had looked at the dark smear of blood on the packed earth where Ricardo's body had lain. Now he stood for a long moment without speaking, his eyes resting first on Regina, then on Solomon, as though trying to read in their faces what his heart already feared. "Tell me," he said at last, his voice low and steady, "exactly what happened." The room thickened with silence. Regina felt her mother's hand pause against her arm, then withdraw. For a heartbeat she considered remaining quiet, letting the accident stand as an accident, but the memory of Ricardo's hands on her, the sour heat of his breath, rose up with such force that she found herself speaking before she could tame the words. She told him everything the way Ricardo had blocked her path near the wall that morning, the warning in her mother's eyes at noon, the pleading in Solomon's voice when he begged her to see Valentino, the foul suggestion in Ricardo's tone as he stood too close in the fading light. She described his grip on her wrist, the unwanted press of his body against hers, the drunken kiss bruising her cheek, the terrible moment when she had blurted out that Jewish girls waited for marriage, and the way his face had twisted when the word "Jewish" hung between them like a curse. She did not spare herself, nor did she shield Ricardo; she spoke as plainly as she could, though several times her voice faltered and she had to stop to breathe. Her father listened without interruption, his hands clasped behind his back, his features rearranging themselves into a mask of aching sorrow and helpless anger. When Regina reached the moment where Ricardo had hurled her into the hay, she felt her throat close, and it was her mother who quietly supplied the next words: "Solomon opened the stall." All three adults turned toward the boy. Solomon's eyes filled with tears, and he shook his head violently, as if denying his own hands. "He was hurting Bu," he whispered at last, his words barely audible. "Valentino was locked in. I wanted him to be free. I didn't know he would... I didn't know..." Regina rose and crossed the room, pulling her brother into her arms. "You were trying to help me," she said, resting her chin on his hair. "You didn't do anything wrong." Her father exhaled slowly, the sound shaky despite his effort to control it. "No," he said in a flat, tired voice. "The wrong was done long before that latch was lifted." He looked away then, toward the narrow window from which a single strip of dying daylight still slipped into the room. "But the world will not see it that way." Her mother, who had remained uncharacteristically quiet, now drew herself up with a kind of defiant calm. "We have already decided," she said. "No one must know what happened in that stable. We will say Valentino panicked; that Ricardo slipped; that the horse reacted. The servants saw only the end of it. They will repeat what we tell them." Her father's eyes returned to her sharply. "And if the boy talks?" "Solomon will say nothing," she replied, glancing at her son with a look that was both plea and command. “And our daughter will say nothing. Not because they are liars, but because we have no choice. If we speak the truth, the truth will kill us.” Regina felt the weight of those words settle on her shoulders like an extra garment. She understood, with a clarity as cold as well water, that her honor, her safety, even her life might depend not on testimony but on silence. In another world, perhaps, she could have gone to a magistrate, could have spoken of the assault and been believed. In this world the law belonged to men who wore crosses on their chests and suspicion in their eyes, men who needed only the faintest rumor of Jewish defiance to ignite the fires of accusation. “What about Ricardo’s family?” she asked, her voice softer now. “Will they not demand an explanation?” “His aunt and cousin will demand many things,” her father said wearily, “but explanations will not be among them. They will want coin for his care, and they will want someone to blame for his misfortune. That someone must not be you. Nor Solomon. Nor any of us.” The idea of paying money to the man who had tried to violate her made Regina’s stomach churn, yet she understood the cruel reasonableness of her father’s suggestion. Money, unlike truth, sometimes satisfied anger; coin could speak in places where words were dangerous. “We will send something,” her mother said, already thinking ahead. “A nurse for a few days, perhaps, and some extra grain for their household. We will say it is in gratitude for his work on the estate. If we appear generous, perhaps they will suspect us less.” Her father inclined his head, though his eyes remained troubled. “Even so, gossip will travel faster than any cart. One of the workers will whisper to another; someone will mention that Ricardo was seen near you earlier in the day, that you quarreled. A story will grow where we cannot see it, like mold in the dark.” “Then we must pray,” her mother replied simply, “that Heaven remembers who spoke the first cruelty and who did the first violence, and that men do not find the courage to ask questions they do not truly wish answered.” The conversation ended not because there was nothing left to say, but because none of them could bear to push further into that dark tangle of possibilities. Solomon was sent to bed with a cup of warm milk; Regina retreated to her chamber, where her mother gently braided her hair for the night as she had done when she was a child. They spoke of small, ordinary things how the olives were ripening well this year, how Hanna had learned a new melody for a Sabbath song as if clinging to these details might anchor them to a future in which this day would recede into memory. When the candles were finally extinguished and the house surrendered to sleep, the sounds of the estate changed. The horses shifted in their stalls; a dog barked once, then settled again; a distant owl called from the grove. Regina lay awake listening, feeling every pulse of her own heart as if it were trying to beat its way out of her chest. Each time she closed her eyes she saw again the moment when the stall door flew open and the black bulk of Valentino surged forward, saw the flash of Ricardo's face turning from arrogance to horror, heard the crack of bone beneath the hammer of the stallion's hooves. She found herself whispering a fragmented prayer not for Ricardo, though she knew she ought to, but for the fragile barrier that still kept the world from knowing precisely what had happened between them. In another part of the countryside, not far beyond the olive groves and the low hills, a very different kind of vigil was taking place. Ricardo lay on a pallet in the dim back room of his aunt's cottage, the air thick with the smell of blood, sweat, and cheap wine used too freely as both medicine and consolation. The village medic had done what he could: he had bound the broken ribs, tried to set the ruined cheekbone, and muttered a few words about the spine that sounded suspiciously like a confession of impotence. When he left, he had shaken his head in a way that suggested the young man would never again rise as he had once leaped onto a horse's back. For long hours Ricardo drifted in and out of consciousness, his mind floating somewhere between pain and feverish dream. Whenever he surfaced enough to recognize the cracked ceiling above him or the lined face of his aunt bent over his bed, rage surged through him with such intensity that even the weight of his injuries could not suppress it. At first the images came jumbled the gleam of Valentino's eye, the sensation of f lying backward, the explosion of light behind his own eyes but gradually they rearranged themselves into a single, burning narrative. He remembered Regina's slap, the sharp sting across his face; remembered the word "Jewish" spat from her lips like an accusation when, in his mind, it was she who should have begged him for mercy; remembered the terror in her eyes as the horse charged and the wild satisfaction he had felt for one brief second when he thought Valentino would stop short and leave her cowering at his feet. The fact that the stallion had struck him instead, crushing his body and his pride, transformed that satisfaction into a hatred he had never before known himself capable of. "She did this," he rasped when his aunt pressed water to his lips. "That girl. The senhorita from the big house. She tempted me, then she set the devil's horse upon me." His aunt crossed herself reflexively, torn between fear of sinning by gossip and the irresistible pull of scandal. "Hush, Ricardo," she murmured, though her eyes were bright with curiosity. "Everyone says it was an accident. You know how that beast is." "Accident?" he snarled, his voice cracking. "She provoked me, then called me filth, then her idiot brother loosed the stallion. All of them are witches, I tell you. Witches and... and Jews." The last word slipped from his tongue with a venom that surprised even him, but the effect on his aunt was immediate. She stiffened, eyes widening, fingers tightening around the rosary that hung from her belt. It was one thing to whisper that the wealthy family who owned the estate kept peculiar customs; it was another to hear the suspicion spoken plainly by someone who believed he had been harmed by them. "Lie still," she said, though her voice had changed. "I will send for the priest. He will know what to do." By the time dawn began to lighten the edges of the sky, a message had already been dispatched to the parish house where Father Alfonso slept behind stone walls warmed by the church's modest tithes. The messenger a narrow-shouldered boy eager for coins carried with him not only the plea that the priest come to bless an injured man, but also the first wild rumors of what had happened on the Nunez Vas estate: that the proud farmhand had been seduced and then betrayed; that the stallion had been unleashed in vengeance; that beneath their thin shell of Catholic respectability the family hid the dark stubbornness of Jews. Gossip, once loosed, travels faster than any horse. It slid through the village before sunrise, growing barbs as it went. By the time Father Alfonso buckled his sandals and prepared to ride out to the cottage, he had already heard enough fragments to feel a twinge of something he would have called righteous concern and others might have named hunger. The Church rewarded those who brought forth hidden heresy. A wealthy household caught in a scandal involving secret Judaism could mean favor, recognition, perhaps even a summons from men who wore the crimson of the Holy Office. On the Nunez Vas estate, however, the morning broke with deceptive normalcy. The servants rose, the ovens were stoked, the animals fed. Regina joined her mother in kneading the dough, their hands moving in practiced rhythm. Yet beneath the surface of every gesture lay the knowledge that something irreparable had happened. The earth beneath them had shifted, even if no one could yet see the fault lines. When her father entered the kitchen with the day's tasks already on his tongue, he paused as if about to speak, then simply kissed his wife's forehead and rested a hand briefly on Regina's shoulder. In that simple contact she felt both his pride in her courage and his torment over the danger it had brought upon them. "We will continue," he said quietly. "We will work, we will smile, we will keep the Sabbath as we always have. And we will trust that the Almighty, who saved our people in lands far from here, will save us again." Regina wished she could borrow his faith as easily as she felt his touch, yet a part of her remained knotted with unease. She had the sense, deep and unshakable, that somewhere beyond the hills and the vineyards, forces were already shifting in response to what had happened in that dim stable. A man whose spine had been shattered would not easily accept his fate as mere mischance; a world that hunted Jews would not ignore a story that placed a converso girl at the heart of a scandal. Still, she shaped the loaves, laid them gently on the board to rise, and whispered the blessing under her breath in the old words her family used only among themselves. The dough swelled soft and obedient beneath the cloth, as if promising a future Sabbath yet to come. Outside, a priest was already on his way to a cottage where a broken man waited with a story sharpened by pain and hatred, and with that story the first true spark of the fire that would soon consume Regina's world.

CHAPTER 4 THE PRIEST & THE CONSPIRACY

The sun had barely lifted itself over the low hills when Father Alfonso rode out from the rectory, his cloak snapping behind him like the wing of a restless crow, the hooves of his mule striking the earth with a rhythm that seemed impatient for trouble. He was a man who moved through the world with the precise arrogance of someone who believed that divine justice wore his face and his voice, and his narrow hands gripped the reins with the pious tension of a man preparing himself for righteous work. The villagers watched him go with a mixture of awe and quiet resentment, knowing from long experience that a visit from the priest could bring blessings but could just as easily bring ruin, for Father Alfonso was not a shepherd who gathered lost sheep but a hawk who sought shadows, convinced that every rustle hid a serpent. The path to Ricardo Castelhano's aunt's cottage wound through low shrubs and dusty olive groves, each twisted tree leaning slightly as though listening to the approach of authority. The cottage itself, with its sagging roof and crooked chimney, sat hunched at the edge of a small pasture like an old woman guarding her secrets. When Father Alfonso dismounted, he took a moment to smooth his robes and compose his expression into one of solemn gravity, though beneath that practiced mask something flickered an eagerness sharpened by the rumor that had reached him before dawn, a rumor hinting that the wealthy family on the hill, the family that lived just a little too quietly and prayed just a little too privately, might finally have revealed their true nature. Ricardo lay inside the dark, cramped room that smelled of damp straw, stale wine, and the metallic stench of blood drying on cloth. His body, broken in several places, seemed little more than a twisted shadow of the arrogant young man who had strutted about the estate only yesterday. His aunt hovered near him wringing her hands, looking at the priest as though he were the answer to a prayer she had not known how to speak. When Father Alfonso touched the threshold, Ricardo's eyes snapped open with a feverish brightness, and the priest saw immediately that the young man's suffering, instead of humbling him, had inflated his bitterness until it burned like a coal beneath the skin. "My son," the priest said, stepping into the room with a measured solemnity that made even the dim air feel heavier, "I have come to hear your confession and offer counsel. They say a terrible accident befell you at the estate." At the word "accident" Ricardo let out a sound that might once have been a laugh, but it cracked in the middle and curdled into a rasp of hatred. He turned his swollen face toward the priest, and though one eye was purpled and nearly sealed shut, the other glinted with a dangerous clarity. "Accident," he repeated slowly, as though savoring the absurdity of the word. "Is that what they are telling you? That it was an accident?" Father Alfonso lowered himself onto the rickety stool beside the bed with deliberate patience, folding his hands in his lap, creating the impression that he was ready to absorb whatever ugliness or truth might spill forth. "That is what the estate claims," he answered, adjusting the cross that hung from his neck. "But you must tell me, Ricardo. You must tell me what truly occurred." And Ricardo, who had been waiting perhaps dreaming for someone to ask, seized the moment with the desperation of a man who felt his dignity slipping into the abyss. He began to speak in a voice raw with pain, and the words poured from him in a feverish torrent. He claimed that Regina Nunez Vas had lured him to the stable with soft looks and secret smiles; that she had begged him to meet her alone; that she had promised him favors no honorable girl would dare speak aloud. Then, he said, when he responded like any man would, she had rejected him, taunted him, called him filth, called him an animal unworthy even to touch her; and when he, overcome with shame and confusion, had confronted her about her cruelty, she had struck him and commanded her simple-minded brother to set the stallion upon him like a demon. He spoke these lies with such conviction, mixing fragments of truth with the poison of his imagination so smoothly that even the rafters of the room seemed to lean in, listening, absorbing the venom one breath at a time. His aunt clutched her rosary so tightly that her knuckles whitened, whispering prayers with a fervor born more from fear than devotion. Father Alfonso did not interrupt once. He let the story unfurl like a tapestry, each thread twisting toward the one conclusion he had already been prepared to accept. When Ricardo finished, panting from the effort of both speech and fury, the priest stared at him for a long, heavy moment, as though weighing the story in his hands. "You say the girl tempted you," he murmured finally, his voice soft, dangerous. "And that she and her brother acted with malice, with deceit, with unnatural cunning." Ricardo nodded, swallowing hard against the pain. "She is not what her family pretends to be. None of them are. They live a lie. They are Jews in secret. I know it. Everyone knows it." The room seemed to vibrate with the force of that accusation. Even the aunt gasped softly, crossing herself again and again, though she did not contradict him. The priest rose slowly, as though the weight of what he had learned pressed upon his shoulders with divine heaviness, but in truth his heart beat faster with excitement. For years he had suspected that the Nunez Vas family harbored heretical customs, that their late night disappearances and peculiar dietary habits signaled something more than eccentricity. Now, with Ricardo's story twisted, embellished, and sharpened by rage he felt the pieces fall into place. "This," he said quietly, "must be brought to the attention of those who safeguard the purity of our land." Ricardo's lips twisted into a satisfied smile. Before the priest left, he promised to pray for Ricardo's healing, though in truth he prayed for something else entirely: for recognition, for advancement, for the opportunity to deliver a prize the Holy Office would not ignore. He rode first to the estate of Senhor Montalvo, the local nobleman whose authority in matters of justice stretched across the villages like a shadow. The nobleman was a tall, gaunt man with eyes that resembled polished stone, a man who had lost his faith in everything except power. When Alfonso recounted the story, embellishing it still further, describing Regina as a temptress, Solomon as a violent "half-wit" trained in the dark arts, and the entire family as secret practitioners of forbidden rites, Montalvo listened with a stillness that was more chilling than anger. In a room lit only by a single oil lamp, the priest and the nobleman spoke for nearly an hour. When they emerged, the verdict had already been decided as effortlessly as if they were choosing a new wine for supper. The Nunez Vas estate would be seized. The family would be charged with heresy and deceit. And Regina seventeen, dutiful, modest Regina would be arrested, tried, and executed by public order. Not because the evidence was sound, or because the accusations were just, but because fear and greed and hatred had woven themselves together into a noose that dangled above her head, and no one in power wished to cut the rope. As the priest mounted his mule once more, the last light of the day bleeding across the sky like a wounded banner, he felt almost holy with purpose. The inquisitorial machine had been set in motion, and he, its humble servant, would guide it toward the family who had dared to hide their faith beneath Portuguese silk. And far away in the Nunez Vas home, Regina sat at her mother's table mending a torn apron, unaware that the world she knew was already collapsing in silence, collapsing faster than an olive branch crackling in the flames.

CHAPTER 5 FLIGHT AND SEPARATION

Night had always been a time of comfort in the Nunez Vas household, a veil under which they could whisper ancient prayers and restore themselves with the fragile peace forbidden to them in the light of day. Yet on this night the darkness pressed upon the house with unusual heaviness, as though the very air carried a warning. Lamps burned lower than usual, shadows thickened in corners where they did not belong, and the simple act of breathing felt strangely labored, as if the house itself knew that something unseen approached its walls with hostile intent. Regina sensed it first not through any sound or sight, but in the way her father paced the length of the dining room with a gravity that made the floor tremble subtly beneath his steps. He rarely paced; he was a man of contemplative stillness, his mind always searching for order in a world that offered none. But tonight he moved as if chased by thoughts too dire to sit with. His lips pressed into a thin line, his eyes fixed not on his children but on the door, the windows, the black smudge of sky beyond the shutters. Her mother, usually the voice of caution, did not chide him or urge him to sit. She too stood rigid, arms folded tightly, gaze flicking again and again toward the small chest in the corner where their most precious objects Sabbath candlesticks, her father's worn siddur, the three hidden manuscripts he had copied by hand were stored. Regina saw her mother's fingers twitch with the impulse to run to them, to gather everything dear before it could be lost, but she held herself still, waiting for her husband to speak the words they all feared he would. It was Solomon who finally broke the silence. He sat on the low stool where he often sorted beans with clumsy earnestness, but now his hands moved aimlessly, picking up one bean only to put it down again. His brow was furrowed with the simple, intuitive worry that came so naturally to him. "Papa," he whispered, "why are you walking so fast? You will get dizzy." Their father stopped, closed his eyes a moment, then knelt beside the boy and cupped his face gently.

"My son," he murmured, "sometimes a man must listen to the ground as much as to the sky. And tonight the ground is telling me that danger is on its way." Regina's pulse quickened. "You heard something?" He opened his eyes, and the depth of sorrow in them made her heart twist. "Not a sound. Not a message. But I feel it. As surely as I have ever known anything." Their mother swallowed hard. "Then it is time." Those three words shattered the last illusion that this was merely a troubled night. They were words reserved for the unthinkable, for the scenario they had prayed never to face: the moment when shadows lengthened and boots approached and the Inquisition or those who wished to please it came to drag Jews from their homes under the cover of darkness. Regina rose from her chair slowly, feeling as though her body were moving through water. "What must we do?" Her father stood, his decision already fully formed. "We leave. All of us. Now." Her mother went at once to the small chest in the corner. She opened it with shaking hands and began pulling out the few items they could not abandon her father's quills and inkpot, the manuscripts wrapped carefully in linen, the candlesticks worn smooth by years of hidden Sabbaths. Regina joined her, retrieving the small pouch of coins they kept hidden beneath the floorboard. She tucked it beneath her sash with a steady hand she did not feel. "Where will we go?" Hanna whispered, rubbing sleep from her eyes as she stumbled into the room, confusion clouding her innocent face. She clutched her wooden doll to her chest, the one Regina had carved for her the previous year. Her mother gathered Hanna into her arms and kissed her hair. "Quiet now, little dove. We are only taking a small journey." But Regina saw the truth in her mother's eyes: this was no journey. It was an escape, a flight from a world collapsing around them. Their father moved quickly through the house, extinguishing lamps one by one, creating a safe pocket of darkness where they could finish packing. "We must separate," he said, his voice soft but firm. "Traveling together will draw too much attention. And if they are hunting us " "They will hunt us," her mother interrupted, clutching the manuscripts to her chest. "We must not pretend otherwise." Her father nodded. “If they hunt us, we must not give them all of us at once.” The air left Regina’s lungs. “Separate? Papa, we cannot leave one another.” He turned to her, the sadness in his eyes gentler than the fear. “My daughter, if we stay together, we will all be lost. But if we divide, some of us may yet survive to tell our story, to carry our name to safer soil.” Regina felt her throat tighten. “Papa...” He stepped forward and took her hands in his, holding them with a tenderness that nearly broke her. “You are our strength, Regina. The men chasing us will not look twice at a young woman traveling alone. They expect men to lead, not girls. That is our shield tonight.” With that he placed his hand on her head, and said: the priestly blessing which fathers and mothers bless their daughters; Yevarechecha Ya’er Hashem Hashem panav ve’yishmerecha. eilecha vi’chuneka. Yisa Hashem panav eilecha ve’yasem lecha shalom. Translated: May God make you like Sarah, Rebecca, Rachel, and Leah. May Hashem bless you and guard you. May Hashem shine His face upon you and show you grace. May Hashem lift His face toward you and grant you peace. Her mother placed a hand on Regina’s, head and gave her too the blessing. Then she put her hand on shoulder. “We have arranged a carriage through Manuel, the tanner’s brother. He owes your father a debt. It waits at the far bend of the road. You will take it north.” “But where will you go?” Regina asked, nearly choking. “We will travel east, toward Spain,” her father said. “Your mother and Hanna will go quickly, on foot through the old vineyard road. I will take the southern path, so that if anyone follows, they will follow me.” “And Solomon?” Regina whispered. Her mother’s breath hitched. “Solomon will go to Rabbi Yehuda’s home. His wife is kind. His house is hidden among the fig trees where no one looks twice. He will be safe.” She looked at her son, smoothing his hair. “You will be brave, meu anjinho. You will stay with the rabbi until we send for you.” Solomon stared at them all with wide, bewildered eyes, as if trying to comprehend why everyone looked suddenly as though they were dissolving before him. “I don’t want to stay with the rabbi,” he said softly. “I want to stay with Bu. I want to stay with Mama.” Regina knelt and held him tightly, feeling his small body trembling against hers. “You will stay with the rabbi only for a little while,” she lied with a gentleness that made her heart crack. “And I will see you again. I promise it with all my soul.” But the look in her father’s eyes told her that promises were all they had left, and even those were as fragile as the thin glass of an oil lantern. They moved swiftly then. Her father lifted Solomon into his arms, murmured the blessing given to boys: Yesimcha Elokim ke-Ephraim ve’chi-Menashe. Yevarechecha Adonai Ya’er Adonai ve’yishmerecha. panav eilecha va’yichuneka. Yisa Adonai panav eilecha ve’yasem lecha shalom. Translated May God make you like Ephraim and like Manasseh. May Hashem bless you and protect you. May Hashem shine His face upon you and show you favor. May Hashem lift His face toward you and grant you peace. Then he slipped out through the side door toward the fig orchard. Her mother clutched Hanna and the manuscripts and hurried through the back gardens toward the old vineyard path. Regina, carrying only a small bundle with a change of clothes, her mother’s herbs, and a tiny folded cloth containing the last damask she had woven, stepped into the hush of the night alone. She paused at the gate, turning once to look at the house that had sheltered her life. The moonlight fell across its whitewashed walls with such quiet beauty that for a moment she allowed herself to believe it was only an ordinary night, that she would return at dawn and find everything as it had been. But something inside her knew she would never cross its threshold again. The wind shifted, carrying with it the faintest sound distant hoofbeats, moving fast. Her father had sensed correctly. The hunt had already begun. Regina turned away from the only home she had ever known and walked into the darkness, her footsteps steady, her heart pounding, and the name Nunez Vas burning within her like a hidden flame she would protect with her life.

CHAPTER 6 REBECA ON THE ROAD

The road that carried Regina away from the estate did not begin as a road at all, but as a narrow, uneven track carved into the earth by generations of shepherds and wandering traders. In daylight it appeared harmless, even ordinary, but beneath the thin wash of moonlight it felt like an uncertain thread connecting the life she had just fled with the precarious, undefined expanse that lay before her. She stepped onto it with the tentative weight of someone who understood that each footprint was not merely a footprint, but a quiet declaration that she no longer belonged to the place she had called home since birth. The driver Manuel's brother, though Regina never learned his name did not speak after she climbed into the carriage. He flicked the reins with the economy of a man used to performing difficult tasks without being thanked for them, and the horse pulled forward with a heavy sigh, as though even the animal felt the burden of the night's urgency. The wheels groaned softly under the weight of the wooden frame, and the old lantern hanging from the side swung weakly, casting a pale wavering glow across the roadside shrubs. Regina wrapped her cloak tightly around her shoulders, not because of the cold, but because she felt that if she left any part of herself exposed, the night might swallow it. Her hands trembled as she clutched her bundle two linen shifts, the pouch of herbs, the small folded damask objects of no worldly value, yet immeasurably important to her because they held a trace of the life that had dissolved only hours earlier. She tried to steady her breathing, but each inhale felt ragged, and each exhale carried the weight of memories she was not yet prepared to release. The estate receded behind her until it was no more than a cluster of faint lights in the distance, then until it disappeared entirely behind a curve in the land. And with its disappearance came the first true ache of separation an ache so deep and sudden that she closed her eyes against it, as if darkness could soften the edges of grief. She thought of her mother's hands smoothing

Hanna's hair, of her father's silent blessing as he placed Solomon into the rabbi's care, of the quiet creak of the olive press near the barn that always sounded just before dawn. These small, living details pressed against her heart with more force than any dramatic farewell could have. She could not cry. Tears belonged to safety, to endings that allowed for mourning. This was neither. Hours passed. Sometimes the road dipped into hollows where the air grew moist and cool, carrying the scent of river reeds; at other times it rose toward ridges from which Regina glimpsed distant valleys dotted with the ghostly silhouettes of farmhouses. Each village they passed seemed to sleep lightly, as though aware that something was amiss in the world. Dogs barked in restless bursts. A shutter banged behind a closed window. Somewhere a rooster, confused by the moon, crowed at the wrong hour. When dawn finally pried a thin line of pale gold across the eastern horizon, the driver halted the carriage at the outskirts of a small, unremarkable settlement surrounded by parched fields. He stepped down without ceremony and gestured toward a low structure with a sagging roof. "You go there," he said. "He's waiting." Regina descended from the carriage with stiff legs and followed where he pointed. The air smelled faintly of dry earth and smoke from early morning cooking fires. A dog wandered across the road, glanced at her without interest, and disappeared behind a haystack. Inside the dim house, the forger was already seated at his table, surrounded by parchments, seals, and inkpots. He did not ask her name; he merely studied her with the dispassionate gaze of someone who has seen grief wear countless faces. He motioned for her to sit, then pulled one sheet of parchment toward him. "You will need a new life," he said, dipping the quill into ink. "Tell me only what must be preserved. Everything else will be rewritten." Regina hesitated. Her true name sparked within her chest, the last ember of the life she was trying to protect. She felt that if she spoke it aloud here this cramped room smelling faintly of damp and ink she might lose it forever. "My father chose the name," she finally whispered. "Rebeca, Rebeca Vas-Dias." He nodded, already forming the letters, each stroke precise and practiced. "Your age?" "Seventeen." "Origin?" Her pulse quickened. Here she would sever the final tie to the land that had nurtured her. "Coimbra," she said quietly. "My parents died when I was young." He wrote without lifting his eyes, crafting the lie with the calm of a man accustomed to replacing painful truths with necessary fictions. When he finished, he sealed the document with red wax and pressed a small metal emblem into it. Regina accepted the paper with both hands, though it felt strangely heavy, as if its weight came not from parchment but from the sheer immensity of what it represented: the deliberate unmaking of her past. When she stepped outside, the sky was a pale shell of morning. The carriage and driver were already gone, leaving her alone at the edge of a world she did not yet know how to navigate. She walked north because north was where her father had once spoken of distant cities where Jews lived without whispers, where Sabbath candles burned openly behind windows rather than in forgotten corners, where names did not have to be hidden beneath borrowed identities. For the first few days, she relied on the rhythm of walking to anchor herself. The steady pattern of her footsteps heel, toe, heel, toe became a kind of mantra that kept her fear from spiraling into panic. Villages rose and fell behind her with indistinct sameness: clusters of whitewashed houses, wells in the center squares, the murmured greetings of peasants who looked at her with curiosity but asked no questions. She learned quickly how to move through these places as a shadow not so invisible as to arouse suspicion, yet not so present as to invite interest. She offered herself for work wherever she found it: scrubbing floors in a tavern whose owner eyed her with coarse amusement; trimming grapevines for a widower who paid her with a handful of figs and a place to sleep in his barn; mending shirts for a carpenter whose wife pressed bread into her hands with motherly gentleness. These encounters, fleeting and simple, did not erase the hollow within her, but they filled its edges just enough to keep her moving. As the months turned to seasons, the landscape around her changed. The scorching heat of summer burned her skin until it browned. Autumn winds sharpened the air and rattled the last leaves from the trees. Winter came early one year, and she endured several nights so cold that she believed she might not wake from sleep, curling herself around her bundle as though it were the only warmth she had left. Still, she walked. And in each town, before each sunset of the sixth day, she sought a quiet place where she could whisper the ancient blessings of Shabbat. Sometimes she crouched behind hedges; other times she hid in abandoned mills or grain storage huts. She had no candles, but she imagined them two slender flames standing like sentinels against the encroaching darkness. She whispered blessings through trembling lips, filling the silence with the last intact pieces of her identity. It was on one of those Fridays several years into her journey that she first felt the faint stirring of hope again. She had reached the outskirts of a port city, where the air smelled of salt and tar and distant lands. She saw, for the first time in years, a small group of men whose faces bore the familiar traces of Sephardic lineage olive skin, dark hair, solemn eyes that seemed to carry centuries. They spoke Portuguese among themselves, not with the rough cadences of peasants, but with the dignified rhythm of families who once lived near courts and academies. They were refugees. She knew it instantly, the way a lost bird recognizes its flock even before it hears their call. She never approached them fear kept her distance intact but she watched them from afar, and something inside her shifted. If refugees could reach the northern ports, then perhaps she could, too. And so, when spring melted the frost from the fields, she set her sights farther north, following the road that wound like a pale ribbon through valleys, villages, and dense forests. It was a journey without maps, without guidance, without any assurance that she would survive it. Yet she walked as though compelled by a force greater than herself by duty, by memory, by the faint but persistent belief that the God of her ancestors had not abandoned her. And one day, after years of wandering, she reached the gates of Amsterdam. It rose before her like a revelation: a city of tall, narrow houses with gabled roofs reflected in glistening canals; a city where merchants from every corner of the world carried spices, books, fabrics, and ideas; a city whose streets hummed with a vibrancy she had never encountered. The smell of cinnamon and pepper mingled with the scent of water and coal. Horses trotted across cobblestones. Bells chimed from church towers. Ships creaked gently in the harbor. And most astonishing of all she saw, woven into the tapestry of this city, men and women who walked openly as Jews. Some wore modest garments embroidered with the motifs of Iberia. Others carried books with Hebrew lettering. Some even lit candles in windows visible from the street, their Sabbath light shimmering without fear. Regina stood at the edge of the canal, her breath catching in her throat. For the first time since she had left her family, she felt the weight of exile loosen just a little. She did not yet know where she would sleep that night, or what work she would find, or how she would present herself in a city where she was both a stranger and someone who longed to reclaim her name. She did not yet know the hardships that awaited her, or the kindness she would soon encounter, or the man whose life would become intertwined with hers in ways she could not yet fathom. But she knew that she had reached the city where her life would begin again. And so, with everything she had carried her pain, her memory, her identity buried under the borrowed name Rebeca Vas-Dias stepped into Amsterdam, unaware that her arrival marked the beginning of a new chapter not only in her life, but in the very legacy of her people.

CHAPTER 7 THE BRINKMEYER HOUSEHOLD

Amsterdam revealed itself to Regina not as a place one simply arrived in but as a labyrinth of waterways, languages, and shifting lights that demanded to be absorbed slowly, with the same careful reverence one would give a manuscript copied by many hands. The canals, narrow and shimmering beneath the restless sky, carried reflections of tall merchant houses whose gabled roofs leaned slightly toward one another as if whispering confidences gathered from winds that had crossed oceans; the streets pulsed with the mingled voices of sailors, Jewish refugees, Dutch shopkeepers, African dock workers, spice traders, and countless wanderers whose footsteps spoke of lands abandoned and futures uncertain. To a girl who had spent years passing through Portugal like a breath that dared not be heard, surviving on silence and borrowed identities, the city appeared at once bewildering and strangely gentle, offering the anonymity of a crowd without the suspicion she had learned to expect, and the noise of commerce without the threat hidden in too much quiet. She moved through it tentatively, as one walks across the surface of a pool whose depths have not yet been measured, afraid that a single misstep a wrong face recognized, a word spoken with the wrong accent might break the illusion of safety and plunge her back into the terror from which she had f led. The first days were filled with hardship. Regina slept wherever darkness allowed: behind a cooper's shop in a shed that smelled of sawdust and tar; in the corner of a spice warehouse beside stacks of burlap sacks; beneath the arch of a narrow stone bridge where the night wind carried the creak of moored boats as if reminding her that the world was wide and restless. Work, though abundant for men, proved elusive for a foreign girl alone; she offered her hands for washing floors, peeling vegetables, carrying bundles, or mending small tears in garments, earning a few coins when she was fortunate and receiving only a crust of bread or the brief warmth of a kitchen hearth when she was not. Yet she learned the city by watching it. She noticed the Portuguese conversos who greeted one another with subtle nods meant to carry meaning without attracting attention; the Spanish women whose shawls were wrapped with the same care her mother had once taught her; the merchants from Recife who carried the scent of sugar and damp earth on their clothes; the elderly bookseller who, believing himself unobserved, brushed dust from the Hebrew volumes hidden beneath his counter; and the faint, familiar hint of saffron drifting from a house where she passed one Friday evening as the sun dipped low, stirring in her a memory so vivid it nearly unsteadied her steps. It was on the tenth morning of her wandering, weary but determined not to surrender to the instability of her new existence, that she found herself near the Bloemgracht canal, where tall warehouses cast long shadows across water that shone like beaten pewter. A small crowd had gathered before the steps of an elegant merchant house, their attention fixed on a servant who was struggling to carry an unwieldy crate up the narrow stone stairway. Regina would have walked past had the crate not tipped dangerously as the servant lost his balance; instinct propelled her forward, and in one swift movement she steadied it with both hands, her weight anchoring it before it could crash to the ground. The servant exhaled, murmuring thanks through labored breath, but before he could continue, a woman's voice cut sharply from inside the doorway, reprimanding him with the authority of one accustomed to being obeyed. She emerged a woman perhaps in her early forties, dressed modestly yet with clear refinement, her dark hair bound neatly in a braided coil, her posture erect and her stride purposeful. She halted the moment her gaze settled on Regina, her eyes narrowing not with suspicion but with the practiced discernment of someone who had learned to read character more swiftly than appearances. "You are not from here," she said at last, not as an accusation but as an astute observation born of long experience. Regina bowed her head slightly in acknowledgment, answering with the respectful restraint she had cultivated for survival. "No, mevrouw." "And your Dutch?" "Learning," Regina said quietly. "Little by little." The woman's eyes traveled to Regina's hands calloused, roughened, carrying the unmistakable imprint of labor and long travel and something in her expression softened almost imperceptibly. She asked whether Regina sought work, whether she knew the discipline required in a household, whether she could read a room by silence rather than words. Regina answered with the humility of one who could not afford pride, yet also with the quiet dignity of someone who had been shaped not only by hardship but by a life once filled with care, learning, and tradition. Finally, the woman stepped aside and gestured inward. "Come in," she said, her tone firm yet not unkind. "A conversation should not be held on the street." Regina hesitated for the briefest instant every instinct warning her against entering any space she did not yet understand but the woman's calm command, and the faint but unmistakable air of integrity in her bearing, reassured her enough to cross the threshold. The interior of the Brinkmeyer house revealed a world Regina had never known, A large Mezuza on the outside of the front door, and on all doors in the house. Further she recognized immediately the order, refinement, and disciplined industry. The air carried the sweet, complex aroma of cinnamon, pepper, and clove; shelves held jars imported from lands she had only heard mentioned in the whispered stories of merchants passing through Portuguese taverns; a harpsichord gleamed quietly in one corner, its polished surface catching the light from tall windows overlooking the canal. In the sitting room, Mrs. Brinkmeyer, having now introduced herself formally asked Regina to tell her name, her family, her intentions. Regina spoke with caution yet truth: she offered her borrowed name without embellishment, admitted to having no family, and asked not for charity but for work. Something flickered in the woman's eyes then not pity, not suspicion, but a clarity that suggested she recognized the fragility of the girl standing before her and the strength required to hide such fragility well. I give charity to those who need, however who works for me, does an honest day of work! and that deserves pay not charity. ," Mrs. Brinkmeyer said in a voice that carried quiet authority, "but I can give labor to one who seeks it honestly. This household demands order, diligence, and discretion. If you can provide that, you will have food and a roof." Gratitude sharp and unexpected rose in Regina's chest, and she accepted with a quiet fervor that needed no elaboration. The attic room where she was installed was small, but to Regina it felt like a sanctuary carved out of the chaos of exile: a narrow bed neatly made, a small window overlooking the canal, and a hook for her cloak all simple objects, yet each one a step toward reclaiming a semblance of life that was neither borrowed nor hunted. She touched the windowsill with a kind of reverence, quietly thanking God for granting her even this small beginning. The following days unfolded with a rhythm she embraced almost hungrily: sweeping floors worn smooth by years of footsteps; arranging linen cupboards according to Mrs. Brinkmeyer's impeccable system; grinding spices in the cellar, where the scents reminded her, with bittersweet sharpness, of her father's teachings about God's presence in the smallest elements of creation; and accompanying her mistress to the market, learning the subtle negotiations between fishmongers, spice traders, and women who guarded their household budgets with fierce precision. Mr. Brinkmeyer, though gentler than his wife, observed Regina with the same quiet discernment. He spent hours in his study recording shipments from Brazil and Morocco, often humming Portuguese melodies that startled Regina not because they were unfamiliar, but because they reminded her of Sabbath afternoons long past. He treated her with polite reserve, as one does when learning whether a newcomer belongs to the fragile machinery of a home. Yet beneath the tranquility of this new order, Regina lived with the constant awareness of her concealed identity, a hidden ember glowing beneath the carefully folded garments in her chest. Whenever she heard Portuguese spoken in the market, tension tightened her spine; whenever a priest passed through the street, she lowered her gaze and felt her pulse race. Each Friday evening, she retreated briefly to her attic, where she lit a tiny, hidden flame beneath her cloak and whispered the ancient blessings that had preserved her through years of wandering. The light flickered against the wooden beams above her, and tears silent, uncontrollable slipped down her cheeks as she prayed for her family scattered across the world. The Brinkmeyer's noticed more than Regina intended. They saw how she returned from her Friday disappearances with a serenity out of place for someone so young and alone; how she whispered words they could not identify but recognized as sacred; how she handled certain objects cloth, spices, candles with the reverence of one carrying centuries of inherited rituals. These small observations gathered gradually in their minds, forming a quiet curiosity and neither wished to voice openly. One afternoon, while Regina was sorting spices in the cool cellar, Mrs. Brinkmeyer paused on the steps above her, watching her with a steady, contemplative gaze. When she finally spoke, her voice held none of the briskness with which she typically issued instructions, but something slower, more deliberate. "Rebeca," she said, "in this city, people come with histories they are unable or unwilling to speak. Some guard their pasts as treasures too delicate to expose them to judgment. Others hide them as wounds that have not yet healed. You do not speak of yours, and I will not force you. But I will say only this: a home is not built solely on dusted tables and orderly cupboards. It is also built on truth, when truth is ready to be spoken." She left before Regina could respond, her footsteps fading up the narrow stairway, and Regina remained motionless for a long while, the weight of the words settling over her like a second cloak heavy, protective, and inescapably true. In the days that followed, Regina understood with growing clarity that secrets, even when kept with skill and necessity, do not remain entirely hidden in a house governed by kindness and intelligence. And indeed, it was not her hesitation or her silences that would reveal her identity to Brinkmeyer's, but something far more intimate: the small, battered prayerbook she kept tucked beneath her mattress, its pages worn soft by her mother's hands and stained in places by her own tears. It was this book the one object she refused to abandon that would, when discovered, betray the name she had concealed and illuminate the story she had tried to bury, ushering in the next chapter of her life with a force neither she nor the Brinkmeyer's could have anticipated.

CHAPTER 8 THE PRAYERBOOK DISCOVERY

Winter settled over Amsterdam with a chill that crept through the narrow alleys and across the waterways, softening the echo of carriage wheels and muting the boisterous calls of the fishmongers along the canals. The Brinkmeyer house, usually humming with the warm scent of cinnamon and cloves, grew quieter as the season pushed daily business indoors. Regina adjusted swiftly to the new rhythms; she rose before dawn to warm the kitchen hearth, carried crates of dried spices from the cellar, and learned to seal the window frames against the biting drafts that sliced through the city like knives of frozen fog. Though she worked with a kind of disciplined serenity that made her presence almost seamless within the household, a faint tension still threaded itself through her daily tasks an anxiety she believed she hid successfully beneath steady hands and lowered eyes. Yet secrecy has its own scent, its own gravity, and even in a house governed by kindness, concealed truths eventually pull the air slightly off-center, drawing the attention of those who know how to observe. It was shortly before Passover a holiday Regina could not celebrate openly, but one she counted toward with the quiet ache of remembrance that the incident occurred. The Brinkmeyer's, like most prosperous households, maintained a tradition of inspecting their home thoroughly before the season, an exercise in order and precision for religious observance, Passover was coming and jews are not to have leavened products in their possession. Mrs. Brinkmeyer approached her task with the same composed intensity she applied to all matters: each room was opened, each chest unlatched, each drawer emptied and examined with an eye trained to detect disorder, waste, or dishonesty. The other maids, accustomed to such scrutiny, hurried to tidy their private belongings before inspection day, hiding the small, pilfered items that the mistress tolerated only when they remained invisible an apple saved from market, a ribbon worn thin but still pretty enough to be considered improper indulgence. Regina, having nothing to hide except the truth of her existence, simply folded her garments neatly at the end of her bed and continued working, believing that as long as her mother's book remained tucked deep beneath her mattress, no one would ever think to look for it. But fate often chooses the quietest moments to shift the course of a life. That morning, the household bustled with activity. Mr. Brinkmeyer examined inventory in the study; the servants scrubbed stair rails and polished brass corners; and Mrs. Brinkmeyer, sleeves rolled back with efficient determination, moved from room to room with a ledger in hand, checking items against her mental map of the household's order. When she reached the attic, where the servants slept, she paused for a moment at the threshold perhaps out of courtesy, perhaps simply to gather breath after the climb before stepping inside. Regina was downstairs, sweeping the corridor, unaware of the footfall ascending the last few steps toward the room where her secret lay hidden. Mrs. Brinkmeyer began her inspection with the calm, methodical gestures of someone long accustomed to managing a large home: she checked the small wooden chest in the corner, the washbasin shelf, the hooks that held aprons and winter shawls. She touched nothing rudely, yet she overlooked nothing. When she reached Regina's bed the narrow pallet tucked neatly beneath the slanted roof beam she pressed her palm along the blanket to smooth it, felt a slight unevenness beneath it, and paused. The movement she made was not one of suspicion but of habit; she lifted the thin mattress just enough to look beneath it, searching only for the forgotten crumbs or scraps that careless maids sometimes left behind. Instead, she found the slim, tightly bound object wrapped in worn linen. At first, she did not touch it. She simply looked at it, her breath drawing in the faintest degree. Then, carefully, as if handling a fragile relic rather than a servant's possession, she lifted the bundle into her hands. The linen unfurled easily, revealing a small prayer book, its leather darkened by years, its spine cracked but lovingly repaired, its edges softened by generations of fingertips. The pages were densely written on thin parchment, in Hebrew and Portuguese, the margins thick with handwritten notes in a woman's delicate script. Mrs. Brinkmeyer even though Jewish even somewhat religious, and observant she did not read Hebrew, but she knew a Jewish text when she held one. Amsterdam was full of them openly printed, openly sold yet this book bore the unmistakable marks of secrecy: the tight wrapping, the hidden place, the emotional wear of pages turned more from longing than routine. She did not call for Regina. She did not announce her discovery. Instead, she closed the prayerbook gently, wrapped it once more in the linen cloth, and descended the stairs with quiet steps. When Regina returned to her attic room later that afternoon and slipped her hand beneath the mattress, the absence of the book struck her like a blow to the chest. Her breath stopped. Then, instinct overpowering thought, she fell to her knees and reached deeper, desperate, certain she had simply misaligned the hiding place. But the hollow space beneath the mattress remained empty. Panic rose swiftly, tightening her throat until she could no longer draw breath. She pressed her hands against her eyes, whispering half-formed prayers, begging God for strength, for understanding, for mercy. If the book had been found, if they knew then everything she had built here, every fragile thread of safety could shatter in an instant. Amsterdam was a haven for Jews, yes, but it was also a place where names mattered, where origins could be traced, where stories could unravel, and where danger, though cloaked differently than in Portugal, could still emerge from the wrong whisper. She forced herself to stand and descend the stairs, her legs trembling. She entered the kitchen where Mrs. Brinkmeyer was arranging jars of newly ground spices on a shelf. The mistress turned as she approached, her face unreadable too calm to reveal accusation, too soft to signal anger. "Mevrouw…" Regina began, her voice breaking despite her attempt at composure. "My book " Mrs. Brinkmeyer lifted a hand, not to silence her but to steer the moment with gentleness. She reached for a small table near the window where, laid neatly upon a folded cloth, rested the prayerbook. Regina's knees nearly buckled. "I found this during the inspection," Mrs. Brinkmeyer said quietly. "I thought it best we speak privately." Regina stared at the book, unable to form words, her hands trembling at her sides. Every instinct screamed to f lee or collapse or fall to her knees in supplication, but the woman's steady gaze held her in place. "You are not who you say you are," Mrs. Brinkmeyer continued, not harshly but with the solemnity of someone stating what was already obvious. "This is no ordinary book. It is well used, well loved, and deeply hidden. And the notes in the margins were written by someone who taught you with devotion." Still Regina said nothing, her breath strained by the force of emotions pressing against her ribs. "I did not show it to the other servants," the mistress added. "Nor to my husband. I brought it to our rabbi." Those words our rabbi struck Regina like a sudden shift of light. Mrs. Brinkmeyer went on, slowly: "He opened it, studied the worn pages, and remarked that the High Holiday sections were almost untouched, while the daily prayers were softened by many years of use. He said only a girl who had no synagogue to attend would pray through such pages with such dedication. He wished to meet you." Regina pressed a hand to her chest, her heart racing so violently she feared she might faint. "Mevrouw... please... I never wished to deceive only to live, to be safe, to " Mrs. Brinkmeyer stepped closer and placed the prayerbook in her hands. The gesture alone made Regina's eyes fill with tears. "You will come to our Shabbat table this week," she said. "You will tell your story when you are ready. Not before. But you must know... you are not alone here. Not anymore." In that moment, something shifted inside Regina something as profound as the first glimmer of dawn after a long, starless night. For the first time since fleeing Portugal, she felt not merely sheltered, but seen. The truth, long held in trembling silence, had begun to surface. And soon, in the glow of Shabbat candles, her real birth name would rise again into the world.

CHAPTER 9 THE SHABBAT OF REVELATION

The hours before Shabbat settled over Amsterdam not as an abrupt shift from labor to rest but as a gradual deepening of atmosphere, a certain stillness that began first in the narrow alleyways where the Jewish merchants folded the last bolts of cloth or weighed the final measures of spices, then in the broad canals whose waters surrendered their restless glitter to the modest hush of early evening, and finally in the tall merchant houses whose windows, catching the diminishing light, seemed to hold within their panes the last instinctive f licker of a fading day. Regina felt this stillness even before she recognized it consciously; it pressed itself softly yet unmistakably upon her senses, and as she moved through the Brinkmeyer household preparing the dining room exactly as Mrs. Brinkmeyer instructed laying the polished silver beside the plates whose delicate rims bore faded traces of blue-and-gold glaze imported from Delft, adjusting the linen tablecloth so that its edges hung evenly over the carved walnut table, checking the wicks of the candles to ensure they would catch flame with dignified certainty she became acutely aware of her own breathing, the slow, measured rhythm of someone who has learned to anticipate danger even in the presence of peace. She had lived too long in the shadow of secrecy not to feel the weight of any transition, and tonight, the shift from weekday existence to Shabbat felt far heavier than anything she had known since coming to Amsterdam. It was not the rituals themselves, familiar to her since childhood in Portugal, nor the tasks she completed with instinctive perfection; it was the knowledge quiet, insistent, and steadily rising that tonight she would stand before strangers, though kind ones, and place her entire life into their hands. She did not yet know why she felt compelled to speak fully, why she sensed that withholding even one thread of her past would betray something essential perhaps the memory of her mother, perhaps the trembling courage of her father, perhaps the fragile soul of her brother Solomon but she understood with an almost painful clarity that silence had served her all the way from Alentejo to Lisbon, from Lisbon to the borderlands, from the borderlands to the nameless roads she had crossed in disguise, yet here in this northern city, silence felt like a garment she needed to remove before it suffocated her completely. Still, as candlelight flickered faintly in the room and the final preparations nearly reached completion, she hesitated. She stood at the window for a moment, gazing out toward the slow-moving canal where the water reflected the melancholy tones of the darkening sky, and felt her heartbeat quicken with a fear that bore no resemblance to the fears she had known in Portugal. Those had been sharp, immediate, localized the fear of being seen by the wrong eyes, of being questioned by the wrong man, of being noticed by a neighbor who might whisper to the priest, of being caught performing a ritual who's meaning the outside world refused to understand. But tonight's fear was subtler and far deeper; it was the fear of exposing her soul after years spent binding it tightly under false names and half-spoken prayers, of laying bare wounds that had never been allowed to heal, of finally voicing aloud the horrors that she had carried alone without allowing them to alter the way her hands worked, the way her face held calmness, the way her voice seldom trembled except in the secrecy of her attic room. The dining room began to fill with the quiet footsteps of Brinkmeyer's, and Regina instinctively straightened her posture, crossing her hands gently before her as she had seen her mother do when confronted with situations requiring both dignity and guardedness. Mr. Brinkmeyer greeted her with the same mild nod he always offered, a gesture that conveyed courtesy and seriousness rather than warmth, while his wife watched Regina with eyes that were keen enough to perceive subtleties yet kind enough not to expose them. A few moments later, the rabbi entered, and Regina felt an involuntary tightening in her chest. He was a man of graceful bearing, neither imposing nor distant, but possessed of a presence that suggested an awareness of human suffering far deeper than anything his measured steps or modest clothing might imply. His eyes held the calm of a man who had seen many wanderers cross the threshold into Amsterdam exhausted from worlds that had shown them little mercy, and yet he carried himself with the dignity of someone who believed not sentimentally, not foolishly that the human soul could still be coaxed toward healing even after enduring unimaginable trials. When the candles were lit and the soft glow illuminated the room with a tranquility that seemed to hush even the murmuring breath of the canal outside, the first blessing was recited over the wine, its words rising with the soothing cadence of a tradition that refused to bow to the centuries of violence arrayed against it. Regina closed her eyes briefly, and in that brief darkness, the memory of her father's voice echoed once more, a faint, distant murmur shaped by fear and love, spoken in the shuttered kitchen of their estate where the single Shabbat candle was hidden inside a clay vessel to shield its light from the watching world. She was still a girl then, unscarred by betrayal, untouched by the rage of men who found their strength in the suffering of others, and unaware that within a few short years, she would stand at the threshold of death more than once. The memory stung, not because it was painful in itself but because it belonged to a world that no longer existed yet was still alive in the deepest recesses of her mind. As the blessing over the challah concluded and the table grew quiet in that peculiar warmth that precedes an act of trust, and they finished the entrée, and the soup, while waiting for the main course: the rabbi turned to her with a gentle, searching gaze. It was not a gaze of interrogation but of invitation an unspoken assurance that whatever she shared would be received not with judgment but with the solemnity that truth deserved. "Regina," he said softly, using her true name, since that was written in the front page of the siddur (prayer book) for my daughter, Regina. For her, this was the first time in her hearing, her real name in years. The Rabbi continued: "when a soul arrives in a new land bearing the weight of many roads, the first act of healing is to be seen. Tonight, if you are willing, let us see you." His words, though tender, fell upon her with the full gravity of a commandment she had avoided obeying for years. She felt her hands tremble slightly, though she clasped them tightly to still their movement. For a moment she could not speak, as if the memories themselves resisted leaving the safety of her silence. But then she drew in a slow breath, and with that breath came a shift small at first, like the loosening of a long-knotted rope, then deeper, like the slow yielding of a door whose hinges had rusted shut. She began with her name. "My name," she said quietly, "is Regina Nunez Vas. I was born in Portugal, in a region where the olive trees bend toward the south and the summers are long and heavy. My family lived as New Christians, but inside our home, we lived as Jews." A faint quiver entered her voice, but she held steady. "We kept Shabbat in secrecy. We whispered blessings behind closed shutters. My father taught us the laws with caution; my mother taught us modesty and silence. My brother Solomon... was gentle, kind, untouched by the malice of the world. And my sister Hanna was still a child, innocent of everything except the softness of our home." She paused, and for a moment her eyes drifted toward the window where dusk had settled fully, turning the canal into a ribbon of darkened glass. The rabbi nodded, encouraging her without prompting her. "I was seventeen," Regina continued, her voice growing firmer, "when a man on our estate Ricardo Castelhano began to take an interest in me. He was a farmhand, strong, coarse, accustomed to commanding animals and believing he could command people as well. My mother warned me to avoid him, but he did not permit avoidance. One evening, in the stables, he tried to force himself on me." Mrs. Brinkmeyer inhaled sharply, but neither she nor her husband spoke. The rabbi listened without blinking, his hands resting lightly on the table, as though steadying the room around her. "I resisted," Regina said simply. "And my brother Solomon, in panic and innocence, opened the stall of our stallion. The animal broke free. Ricardo was trampled." Her voice did not waver as she spoke of the violence; she had carried it too long for trembling to serve any purpose. "He lived," she added, "but not whole. And in his brokenness, he found hatred. A priest Alfonso came to him. A man who despised Jews even more than he desired power. He twisted Ricardo's lies into a weapon. They claimed I seduced him. They claimed my brother summoned demons. They declared us guilty. The verdict was death for me." The candles flickered slightly, though no wind touched them. "My family fled that night," she said. "We separated in the darkness. My father forged documents for me; he gave me the name Rebeca Vas-Dias. My parents fled toward Spain with Hanna. Solomon was left with a rabbi who promised to hide him. I do not know what it became of them. I searched for months, but every road brought rumors, not truth. I traveled through villages where my name was still whispered as a curse, through towns where the smoke of the Inquisition had barely faded, and through borders where the fear of being recognized was constant as breath. The rabbi leaned forward slightly, his eyes reflecting a quiet sorrow. "How did you survive?" he asked. Regina lowered her gaze. "I survived the way all exiles survive," she said. "I disappeared. I worked in kitchens, in fields, in houses where I was treated kindly, and in houses where I was treated no better than an animal. I slept in barns, under bridges, in abandoned sheds. I prayed in silence because speaking aloud felt like drawing a knife across my own throat. And when I finally reached Amsterdam, I arrived with nothing not even my voice." She unclasped her hands then, reaching into the small pocket sewn discreetly into her dress. From it she withdrew the linen-wrapped prayerbook, holding it with the reverence of someone who knew that a few pages of ink and parchment carried more history than any stone building. "This," she whispered, laying it gently on the table, "is the only inheritance that remained to me. My mother's handwriting is in its margins. My tears are in its pages. It is the only witness to my life." No one moved. Even the water outside seemed to hush itself. Regina continued, her voice quieter but stronger: "For years I believed speaking these things would destroy me. But silence has its own destruction. Tonight... I wish to live without hiding." She looked up then, allowing her gaze to move from the rabbi to Mr. Brinkmeyer, then to the mistress of the house whose eyes glistened with the restrained emotion of a woman unwilling to weep before others. The rabbi rose slowly, placing one hand on the table. “Regina,” he said, “you have carried more sorrow than any soul should bear alone. You are among your people now. Your truth is safe here.” Mrs. Brinkmeyer reached across the table and gently placed her hand over Regina’s. “You are no longer alone,” she said, her voice steady. For the first time since the night she fled Portugal, Regina felt something shift inside her not relief, not joy, but a solemn quieting of the storm that had lived in her chest for so long that she had forgotten life could exist without it. She bowed her head, but not in fear. In gratitude. In belonging. And in that moment, beneath the steady glow of Shabbat candles, Regina understood that her life, fractured and scattered though it had been, had finally reached a place where its pieces could be gathered again not perfectly, not without scars, but with the dignity of one who had survived without surrendering her soul.

CHAPTER 10 ADOPTION AND RENEWAL:

Over the weeks that followed Regina's revelation, the Brinkmeyer household moved with a gentleness that felt, to Regina, both bewildering and profoundly unfamiliar, for she had long believed that any truth she spoke aloud would return to her sharpened into a blade. Instead, the truth she had released into the candlelit stillness of their dining room seemed to settle upon the home like a soft layer of evening snow cool, quiet, and strangely protective. Nothing changed abruptly; no sudden gestures of pity or suffocating affection intruded upon her routines. Rather, the entire household appeared to orient itself around her presence with a subtle, nearly imperceptible shift, as though her story had altered the gravitational center of the home without disturbing its structure. Regina rose each morning with the same disciplined punctuality that had guided her in Portugal and on the roads that followed, yet she found that something within her had softened; she no longer woke with the instinctive tension of one anticipating pursuit or punishment. Instead, she experienced a hesitant but unmistakable sense of belonging, as if the walls that enclosed her room once mere physical shelter had begun to absorb fragments of her identity and reflect them back with an acceptance, she had not believed possible. From her small attic window, she watched the fog lift from the canal each morning in pale ribbons, and she wondered with a quiet awe how a city that had once felt vast and impenetrable now seemed to rise around her like a cupped hand. Mrs. Brinkmeyer, for her part, neither questioned Regina about her past nor attempted to draw her into forced intimacy. Instead, she offered her companionship through the steady rhythm of domestic life through the quiet scraping of vegetable peels in the kitchen, the measured steps they shared on the way to the market, the momentary glances exchanged while setting out linens or arranging spices in symmetrical rows. These small interactions, unadorned and devoid of sentimentality, formed a kind of emotional bridge across which both women traveled slowly, each aware that trust grows not through declarations but through the constancy of presence. Mr. Brinkmeyer watched Regina with scholarly patience, as though observing an intricate instrument gradually regaining its capacity to function. He asked little of her beyond her usual duties, yet he often paused in the doorway when she entered a room, as if silently attuning himself to her emotional state. On several occasions, when he returned from the port with the scent of salt air and exotic spices clinging to his clothing, he placed a small parcel on the table nothing extravagant, merely something thoughtful: a length of fabric with a Portuguese weave, a small tin of saffron whose fragrance transported her instantly to childhood memories, or a quill carefully carved in a style reminiscent of the scribes of her youth. He never commented on these gifts, and she never thanked him aloud; gratitude flowed instead through the quiet reverence with which she touched each object. time The rabbi visited the household twice during this period, each engaging in long, contemplative conversations with the Brinkmeyer's while Regina prepared tea in the adjacent room, her ears attuned not to the content of their discussion but to the tone, which carried neither urgency nor alarm. There was something deeply comforting in this restraint. The rabbi never summoned her, never pressed her to recount her story again, never intruded upon the fragile equilibrium that had settled over her. Instead, he treated her continued presence in the house as something natural and unremarkable, a sign that her revelation had placed her not under scrutiny but under protection. Yet for all the gentleness around her, Regina struggled with the quiet storm that lived within her. She felt it in the evenings, when the day's busyness receded and she found herself seated by the attic window with only the distant creak of ships on the canal to accompany her thoughts. It was then that memories rose with an almost physical force memories of her mother lighting the hidden Shabbat candle in Portugal, hands trembling not from age but from fear; of her father's low voice reciting the prayers of a man whose faith had been forced underground; of her sister Hanna's quiet laughter and her brother Solomon's gentle touch. These recollections were no longer sharp with panic but heavy with longing, as though each memory were a stone submerged in deep water. There were evenings when Regina, without fully realizing it, would begin to hum the melodies of her childhood ancient Sephardic tunes carried across generations, their haunting intervals echoing through the darkness. Once, as she descended the stairs carrying a tray of freshly baked pastries, she caught the Brinkmeyer's standing motionless near the doorway, listening to her voice drifting down from the attic. She froze in embarrassment, but to her surprise, they said nothing, offering her instead the kind of smile that acknowledged both sorrow and beauty without reducing one to the other. In time, Mrs. Brinkmeyer broached a subject that Regina had avoided since her arrival: the question of ritual observance. One cold morning, as the two women stood in the kitchen kneading dough with steady, practiced motions, the mistress paused and wiped her hands on her apron before turning to Regina with an expression of restrained sincerity. "I have been speaking with the rabbi," she said, her voice calm but carrying unmistakable intent. "He tells me there are ways to bring a home fully into our tradition, if one desires such a path." Regina felt her breath catch, though she kept her gaze f ixed on the dough beneath her hands. "This is your home, mevrouw," she answered slowly. "It is not for me to " But the older woman raised a hand gently, cutting her off without force. "A home," she said, "is not defined only by the stones that enclose it, but by the lives lived within its walls. If you are to be part of this household, then the question is not what my home is, but what our home may become." The word "our" struck Regina with an intensity that nearly unsteadied her. She had long believed that her identity could survive only in secrecy, that the life she had fled could never be carried openly into any new dwelling, and yet here was a woman offering not only acceptance but transformation. She nodded slowly, unable to speak, and in the days that followed, the Brinkmeyer's, under the rabbi's guidance, began the gradual process of reshaping their home according to the laws of the faith. It was not a sudden overhaul but a deliberate reconstruction, carried out with the dignity of people, reclaiming something essential rather than adopting a novelty. Regina assisted each step of the way, and in doing so, she felt her own identity reawakening tentatively, reverently like an ember long buried beneath ash. She found herself drawn once more to music as well. In the early evenings, after her tasks were complete, she often lingered near the harpsichord standing in the corner of the parlor, its polished surface reflecting the f licker of the candles. At first she touched only the keys, letting her fingers rest upon them without pressing, as though reacquainting herself with an old friend. Eventually, she began to play softly at first, then with increasing confidence drawing from memory the melodies her mother had sung in Lisbon during rare moments of safety. The music seeped through the rooms of the house with an almost sacred hush, and though the Brinkmeyer's never interrupted her, she sensed them listening each time, allowing the notes to weave themselves into the fabric of their lives. Thus weeks passed quiet, steady, and transformative. Only at the end of this slow, deliberate unfolding did the Brinkmeyer's approach the question that had lingered unspoken between them. It happened on an evening when the canal lay still beneath a crescent moon and the silence within the house carried a contemplative weight. Regina had finished her tasks and stood near the fireplace, her hands clasped lightly before her, when Mr. Brinkmeyer entered with an expression of solemn decision. His wife followed, her eyes calm but resolute. "Regina," he began, his tone formal yet infused with an unmistakable tenderness, "your presence in this home has changed it in ways we could not have anticipated. You have brought with you a history that demands reverence and a strength that commands respect. We have spoken much with the rabbi and much with one another, and we believe" he glanced toward his wife, then back to Regina "that it is only right to offer you a place in this family not merely as a member of the household, but as our daughter." Regina felt herself rooted to the floor, unable to respond. Her mind raced back through every moment of exile every night spent shivering in the cold, every road walked without companionship, every whispered prayer spoken into a void where no answer returned and she found herself unable to comprehend how a life built upon flight and abandonment had led her to this moment of belonging. Mrs. Brinkmeyer stepped forward then and took Regina's hands gently in hers. "You do not need to answer now," she said quietly. "We understand the weight of such a decision. But know this: we do not offer charity, and we do not act out of pity. We see you as you are. And we wish to make you part of our family." Tears rose to Regina's eyes, but she blinked them back, not wishing to obscure the faces before her. She searched for words, but only one seemed possible. "Yes," she whispered. And in that whisper, something inside her shifted not with the suddenness of collapse but with the quiet strength of a foundation being laid. The adoption was formalized in the weeks that followed, each step carried out with dignity and gravity. When at last the rabbi pronounced her as "Regina Haya Brinkmeyer's," the name settled upon her not as a replacement for her past but as an extension of it a name that bore the memory of what she had lost and the promise of what she had found. And so, with the passing of winter into early spring, Regina stepped into a new life not free from the shadows that shaped her but no longer defined by them.

CHAPTER 11 SUITORS FOR REGINA

The arrival of suitors into the Brinkmeyer household did not occur as a sudden flourish of activity, nor as a ceremonious acknowledgment of Regina's new place within the family; rather, it began with a subtle shift an adjustment of tone, of posture, of glances exchanged between husband and wife much like the faint cooling of the air that precedes an autumn wind. Regina sensed it long before it was spoken aloud, for she had become attuned to the unspoken rhythms of the house, and she knew that when a family begins to think about the future of a daughter, even an adopted one, a certain careful quietness settles into the corners of conversation, a quietness that is not so much secrecy as preparation. It was during one such moment on a gray afternoon when the sky hung low like an unformed thought that Regina understood the unspoken decision had been made. She was seated near the kitchen hearth shelling almonds, her fingers moving with the steady rhythm of habit, when Mrs. Brinkmeyer entered the room with an expression that balanced delicacy and resolve. The mistress stood for a moment watching the fire, as if selecting her words from its shifting shapes, and then spoke in a tone that attempted to sound casual but failed to conceal its gravity. "Regina," she began, "you know that in our community, when a young woman reaches a certain stage in life, it is customary to consider... companionship for the future." Regina's fingers paused mid-shell, her body becoming still with a tension she wished she could control. Companionship. A word that sounded harmless in other mouths but carried for her a weight both heavy and ambiguous. She lowered her eyes, not in shame but in a deep and instinctive caution. "Yes, mevrouw," she murmured. "We would never press anything upon you," the older woman continued gently. "But some families have expressed interest, or at least curiosity, and the rabbi believes it may be healthy for you to meet with individuals of good standing men who respect tradition and understand the delicacies of your past." At that, something inside Regina recoiled with a suddenness she could not conceal. Not in the form of a visible movement, for her posture remained controlled, but in an internal tightening that constricted her breath, as if her ribs themselves had become a cage. Men of good standing. Respect tradition. Understand delicacies. She had heard those words before not in Amsterdam, not in safety, but in Portugal, where men of "standing" believed they could take what they pleased, and priests who "understood delicacies" twisted innocence into accusation. Her heart pounded with memories she had long kept silent: Ricardo's breath against her cheek, the roughness of his hand, the claustrophobic walls of the stable, the crushing weight of his body, the false accusation that followed, the verdict that condemned her to death. The words "suitor" and "future" intertwined with those memories in a knot so tight she felt she might choke on it. Mrs. Brinkmeyer noticed the shift she was a woman who had spent her life reading the unspoken emotions of others and she stepped closer, placing a gentle hand on Regina's arm. "There is no urgency," she said softly. "And no expectation. Only the possibility of meeting people who might value your strength." Regina nodded, though her breath remained shallow. She wished to speak, to explain the turmoil churning inside her, but the words would not form; they scattered like frightened birds each time she reached for them. How could she explain that the very idea of a man standing too close to her made her stomach twist with dread? That the touch of any stranger might collapse the fragile structure she had built for herself? That her body still carried the memory of violation like a brand pressed into flesh? Yet something else troubled her even more deeply: the guilt she felt for reacting this way, for repelling the prospect of marriage as though it were a threat rather than a promise. Her mother had once spoken of marriage with reverence, describing it as a covenant not merely between two individuals but between families, between past and future. Regina had imagined herself one day stepping into such a bond with quiet dignity. But that was before the stable, before the flight, before fear became woven into the fibers of her being. The first suitor arrived more than a week later a man named David Abenacar, the son of a respected merchant family. He was introduced with the restraint typical of Amsterdam's Sephardic community: no dramatic entrances, no elaborate gifts, no bold displays of wealth. He entered the parlor with a gentle nod, greeted Mr. and Mrs. Brinkmeyer with the courtesy of a well-raised young man, and then turned toward Regina with a polite, measured gaze. He was neither handsome nor unattractive, neither overly confident nor timid. He carried himself with the calm self-assurance of someone who believed he had a future that would unfold predictably according to the customs of his family and community. Regina lowered her eyes as he approached, not out of modesty alone but to shield herself from the intensity of being observed. She felt the familiar tightening in her chest and willed her breath to remain steady. David, unaware of the storm within her, offered a gentle smile. "Miss Brinkmeyer," he said, "it is an honor to meet you." His voice was pleasant controlled, almost scholarly but even this unthreatening tone sent a tremor through her, for it reminded her that male gentleness could be as unpredictable as male violence. Her mind flickered unexpectedly to Ricardo, whose smile had once been pleasant enough to fool even her mother for a time. She forced herself to return David's greeting with a quiet "Good evening" and allowed him to sit opposite her as propriety required. The conversation that followed was harmless. He spoke of his work in his father's trade, his studies in religious law, his admiration for Amsterdam's growing Jewish community. He asked polite questions about her adjustment to life in the city, about her skills, about her interests. Yet every question mild though it was felt to Regina like something near an examination, as though each polite inquiry sought to uncover a part of her she had worked too diligently to protect. Her answers came softly, unadorned, cautious. She watched his hands more than his eyes, studying the way his fingers rested on the armrest of the chair, their movements calm and deliberate. The meeting lasted barely twenty minutes, yet when he left, Regina felt as though she had endured an hour of restrained breath. That night, she could not sleep. She lay awake staring at the wooden beams of her attic ceiling, her breath shallow, her fingers curled into the blanket as though anchoring herself to something solid. Her thoughts circled not around David, who had been nothing but respectful, but around her own body how it stiffened when he spoke to her, how her muscles braced instinctively when his shadow moved across the floor, how the memory of Ricardo's grip tightened around her mind even though years had passed. She despised this reaction. She despised its weakness. She despised that a man she had never met before, a decent man who offered her nothing but courtesy, could provoke such turmoil. Most of all, she despised the realization that she feared not only the wrong men but the right ones too. More suitors came in the following weeks each one respectable, each one well-mannered, each one introduced by the rabbi or by families who admired the Brinkmeyer's. They bore gifts of modest sweetness: a small pouch of cloves from Recife, a silk ribbon, a small book of psalms bound in blue leather. Regina accepted each offering with quiet gratitude, yet inside, she felt as though she were failing some essential test. She wished to feel curiosity. She wished to feel openness. She wished even to feel the beginnings of hope. But instead, she felt something closer to suffocation. Each suitor's presence stirred in her the same cascade of memories: Ricardo's voice whispering in the stable, his hand gripping her waist, the force of his body against hers, the panic in Solomon's eyes, the thunder of hooves, the sickening sound of bone shattering. Every polite question from a suitor echoed as an accusation. Every gentle smile felt like a mask that could be torn away at any moment. Even the respectful distance they kept seemed to echo the distance she had created within herself an emotional chasm she feared no man could ever cross. And yet, beneath all of this turmoil, a quieter fear took root: the fear that she was broken in some irrevocable way, that no matter how much love the Brinkmeyer's offered, no matter how much safety Amsterdam provided, she would remain forever trapped in the stable of her past, unable to allow another human being to draw near without awakening the terror that lay coiled within her like a serpent. As the final suitor of the winter season left the Brinkmeyer house a kind, soft-spoken widower named Isaac Belmonte Regina felt exhaustion so profound it bordered on physical pain. She withdrew to her attic room, closed the door gently behind her, and sat on the edge of her narrow bed, her hands trembling in her lap. She could not name what she felt fear, guilt, shame, grief, all mingled together in confusion so dense she could not pry one emotion apart from another. Below, she heard the Brinkmeyer's speaking softly, their voices rising and falling with thoughtful cadence. They were not disappointed in her; she sensed that they understood more than they spoke. Yet Regina felt she had disappointed some unseen force perhaps her mother's memory, perhaps the future she once imagined. And it was then, alone in the quiet of the attic, that a truth emerged with startling clarity: It was not that she could not love. It was that she had not yet healed enough to allow love to approach her without tearing open wounds that had never fully closed. She pressed her hands over her face and wept not loudly, not violently, but in long, controlled breaths, the kind of tears shed not out of despair but out of the awakening recognition that healing itself is a journey as long and uncertain as exile. The morning after Isaac Belmonte's visit dawned with a pale, water-soft light that diffused through the thin layer of fog suspended over the canal, giving the entire city a muted, introspective calm, as if Amsterdam itself were pausing to consider its thoughts. Regina descended the narrow staircase with her usual careful steps, though her body felt heavier than on other mornings, as though the night had pressed its weight upon her and she had not fully risen from beneath it. Her eyes carried a tense brightness, the kind that comes from a night spent in silent reflection rather than sleep, and her movements, while precise, held the faint tremor of someone who wished to appear composed, but whose inner quiet had been shaken. Mrs. Brinkmeyer was in the kitchen preparing tea, and though she glanced at Regina with her customary warmth, there was a perceptible softness an almost maternal attentiveness in her gaze that told Regina her distress of the previous evening had not gone unnoticed. The mistress said nothing at first; instead, she motioned for Regina to sit at the small table near the window where the early morning light cast a fleeting shimmer across the polished surface. Regina obeyed, folding her hands gently in her lap, though her posture remained controlled, as if she feared that even a slight relaxation might allow emotion to spill over. The silence stretched between them not as a void but as a deliberate space, one that both women recognized as necessary. At last, Mrs. Brinkmeyer set the teapot down with a quiet clink and lowered herself into the chair opposite Regina. "You do not need to pretend with me," she said kindly. Regina looked up, startled by the directness, though the older woman's voice carried no accusation, only understanding. She opened her mouth to respond but found herself caught between several truths, none of which she was prepared to speak aloud. Instead, she exhaled, long and steady, as if releasing a breath she had been holding for weeks. "It is only..." she began, then faltered. She lowered her gaze to her hands, which were folded so tightly the knuckles had grown pale. "I do not know what is expected of me." Mrs. Brinkmeyer reached across the table, her fingers resting lightly upon Regina's. "Only that you try to live," she said. Regina felt the warmth of her touch, gentle and unforced, and the simplicity of the words struck her more deeply than any elaborate reassurance could have. She nodded slowly, though the heaviness within her did not dissipate. For she understood, with a kind of dawning clarity, that the matter was not merely expectation but the painful gap between what she feared she was capable of and what she believed a future demanded. Later that afternoon, after the household tasks had been completed and the canal began to shimmer beneath the glints of a clearing sky, the rabbi arrived at the Brinkmeyer home, having been informed in a quiet manner that Regina was troubled. He asked to speak with her in the small study near the back of the house, a room lined with books whose leather bindings gave off a faint scent of age and dry ink, a scent that reminded Regina of the secret alcove where her father had kept his hidden volumes in Portugal. She entered the room with reserved steps, aware that the rabbi, though gentle, possessed an instinct for perceiving truths concealed even from oneself. He motioned for her to sit in the high-backed chair across from him, and when she had settled, he regarded her with a thoughtful, almost contemplative expression. "I hear," he began, "that meeting the young men of our community has brought you discomfort." There was no judgment in the words, only observation. Regina lowered her gaze. "I do not wish to be ungrateful," she murmured. "They are kind. They are respectful. But I..." She struggled for the right words, for how does one explain fear to someone who has not felt the exact shape of it? How does one describe the way trauma lives not in memory alone but in the body itself how the muscles remember what the mind wishes to forget, how the breath tightens at a man's approaching footsteps even when he is harmless? The rabbi waited patiently, and after a long pause, Regina continued, her voice trembling like a candle flame. "I am afraid that I will never be the kind of woman who can give herself to a man without fear. I am afraid that something in me is broken, that what happened in Portugal has taken from me something I cannot recover." The rabbi nodded slowly, his eyes softening with a compassion that did not pity her but honored the weight of her suffering. "Regina," he said, "there is no brokenness in surviving what you have survived. There is only endurance, and endurance is not the absence of wounds but the courage to continue carrying them. You speak of fear as though it reveals a flaw in your character. But fear, in this case, is a sign of your humanity, not your failure." She swallowed, her throat tight. "But how can I marry," she asked, "if I tremble at the idea of any man drawing near me?" The rabbi leaned back slightly, folding his hands. "There are two kinds of nearness," he said. "The nearness that forces itself upon a person, and the nearness that waits patiently. The first wounds. The second heals. Men like Ricardo impose. Men of true character men of kindness and depth do not invade. They approach. They listen. They wait." He paused, letting the words settle. "And if there comes a man one marked by gentleness rather than entitlement, one who seeks your heart rather than your submission then you may find that the fear which binds you now does not hold forever. Healing is not an instant, Regina. It is a slow awakening." Something in her chest tightened, but this time, not entirely from pain. The rabbi spoke with such calm authority that she felt, for a brief moment, the faintest glimmer of possibility not hope, not yet, but the idea that hope might one day be possible. He continued in a gentler tone. "For now, it is enough that you breathe. That you rise each morning. That you walk through this city with steps that are no longer hunted. The right man, if he is meant to come, will meet you where you are not where fear tells you must be." Regina closed her eyes briefly, letting the words settle like a balm on a wound that had been open too long. That evening, after the rabbi departed and the house grew quiet, Regina walked alone to the attic, her thoughts heavy but clearer than they had been in weeks. She lit her small candle and sat beside the window, watching the moon rise above the rooftops. The canal below glimmered in pale silver lines, and the faint sounds of distant wheels on cobblestone drifted up from the streets, mingling with the quiet rustle of evening wind. She thought of the suitors, of their calm voices and polite gazes. She thought of the rabbi's words, profound in their simplicity. And gradually, she began to understand that her struggle was not a flaw but a journey that the men she had met were not wrong for her, nor was she wrong for them, but that the timing, the emotional distance, the internal turmoil created a chasm she could not yet cross. And in that realization, something softened inside her, a fragile acceptance of her own humanity. Over the next weeks, the Brinkmeyer's respected her silence on the matter. They did not press further; they did not arrange more meetings. Instead, they allowed her to move through her days with measured calm, restoring her sense of safety. But the world, as it often does, had its own plan. One afternoon, as Regina accompanied Mrs. Brinkmeyer to the tailor to adjust new linens for the household, she noticed a young man standing near the edge of the Singel canal, examining architectural sketches with a concentration so complete it seemed to envelop him entirely. His posture was refined, his profile noble, and there was something in the way his eyes moved focused, searching, restless yet controlled that stirred within Regina something unfamiliar, something that did not resemble fear. She glanced only briefly, yet the image stayed with her long after they returned home. She did not know his name. She did not know that he would become the axis around which her world would gradually, quietly turn. She did not know that Rafael Enríquez Diego Toledano had seen her as well only for a moment, yet long enough to sense, without understanding why, that the city around him had shifted its breath. And so, without premonition, without prophecy, without any of the drama that stories often demand, the future entered her life not with the arrival of a suitor, but with the gaze of a man who was not meant to be one at least not yet. That moment, quiet as it was, marked the beginning of the slow, profound, beautifully complex unraveling of all the fears that had bound her. But Regina did not know it. Not yet.

CHAPTER 12 THE YOUNG PORTUGUESE NOBLEMAN

Amsterdam, with all its bustling canals and merchant cries, had always served as a kind of refuge for men and women who had wandered far from the lands of their birth. Yet for some souls the city was not merely a refuge but a stage upon which the remnants of the past converged with the possibilities of the future; and for Rafael Enríquez Diego Toledano, whose life had unfolded in the shadows and splendors of Iberian tradition, the Dutch city had become a place both of exile and of self-discovery. He walked its narrow streets with the posture of a man who bore his lineage not as an ornament but as an inheritance of responsibility, refinement, and quiet sorrow. Rafael was the son of a family that had once breathed the rarefied air of Portuguese scholarship. His father, Don Benjamin Enríquez Toledano, had been a jurist whose evenings were divided between the intricate legal debates of the Talmud and the equally intricate rhetoric of the courtrooms where he once served in secret as an adviser to families who lived beneath the weight of Christian scrutiny. His mother, Dona Miriam, was a midwife of great gentleness and dignity, known for her calm presence in the most delicate hours of a woman's life, and whispered of in the hidden communities that practiced their Jewish rituals beneath locked shutters and bolted doors. Rafael grew up in a household where books were treated as sacred companions, where the rhythm of the day followed both the laws of kings and the laws of Heaven, and where exile was spoken of as a certainty long before it arrived at their doorstep. When persecution tightened its noose around their home, the Toledano family fled toward the North Sea, carrying with them nothing but a few precious volumes, a pair of silver candlesticks, a manuscript of his father's legal writings, and a deep, immovable pride that came not from wealth but from spiritual inheritance. In Amsterdam, Rafael inherited not only his father's knowledge but his temperament: disciplined, introspective, keenly perceptive, and marked by a quiet, unwavering courtesy that made his presence felt without ever announcing itself. By the age of twenty-four he had become known among the Sephardic merchants and scholars of Amsterdam as a gifted designer of canal houses and merchant dwellings. His architectural sketches precise, elegant, and imbued with a subtle poetic sense of proportion had earned him a reputation that crossed the boundaries between Christian merchant households and Jewish ones. He had no desire for notoriety, yet the quality of his mind and the seriousness of his character drew the attention of all who encountered him. It was perhaps for this reason, among others more intimate and intuitive, that the rabbi of the Portuguese congregation summoned him late one Thursday afternoon. Rafael arrived at the study with his usual calm, though he sensed at once that the rabbi's request would be of a more personal nature than the scholarly discussions that typically occupied their time together. "My son," the rabbi began, folding his hands thoughtfully before him, "there is a young woman in our community who carries both sorrow and strength within her in rare measure. She is of Portuguese blood, a girl who has endured much and yet has retained her dignity, her modesty, and her faith. Her name is Regina Brinkmeyer formerly Rebeca Vas-Dias and before that, something she guards with deep caution. Rafael listened with the concentrated stillness that defined him. The rabbi observed him carefully before continuing. "She is the adopted daughter of the Brinkmeyer's. Their home has given her protection, but not yet companionship. She is of marriageable age, but neither her past nor her nature allows her to attach herself lightly. I believe" the rabbi paused, perhaps choosing his words with care "that you might be a man who could meet her without frightening her, without attempting to claim her before understanding her, without confusing gentleness for weakness or silence for simplicity." Rafael lowered his gaze, not out of reluctance but out of the gravity with which he received such matters. "If you think it proper, rabbi, I will visit the household. But I do not wish to intrude on a girl who has already suffered more than should be asked of anyone. “Precisely why I ask you,” the rabbi replied with a small, satisfied nod. “This is not matchmaking in the ordinary sense. It is the careful opening of two lives that may, if Heaven wills it, understand one another.” The next Shabbat afternoon Rafael made his way to the Brinkmeyer residence. The sky above the canal was the color of pewter, the air scented faintly with clove and cinnamon from the spice warehouses that lined the water. The Brinkmeyer home stood tall and dignified, a structure that carried the self-assured symmetry typical of merchant families who had acquired wealth not by ostentation but by steady, honorable trade. Rafael knocked quietly, adjusting his posture with the calm of a man entering not a business meeting but a moral encounter. Mrs. Brinkmeyer herself opened the door, her expression composed yet warm. She greeted him with a manner that combined Dutch restraint with the lingering courtesy of Portuguese upbringing. She led him into a parlor that smelled faintly of sandalwood and dried orange peel, where sunlight filtered through narrow windows, softening the room with a delicate amber glow. And there, arranging a tray of tea with precise, almost reverent motions, stood Regina. Rafael felt a subtle shifting in the air as he observed her not a jolt, not a dramatic spark, but the unmistakable sensation of encountering a person whose presence drew the attention of the mind before the heart had even understood why. She was dressed simply, her hair gathered with the modesty of a woman who neither flaunted nor concealed her beauty, as though she understood deeply that elegance was an inward discipline rather than an outward performance. Her face bore a gentleness that did not diminish its strength; her eyes were dark, serious, and reflective, like a person who had learned early to guard the vulnerable spaces within herself. When she turned to greet him, he noticed the faintest hesitation a moment where her breath seemed to catch, as if she were accustomed to meeting strangers with caution and preparing herself for whatever assumption or misinterpretation they might impose upon her. But Rafael, who had spent his childhood observing the unspoken languages of courts and synagogues, understood immediately that the correct approach was not admiration, nor quick familiarity, but a dignified courtesy that asked nothing and promised nothing premature. “Senhor Toledano,” she said with careful enunciation, “you are welcome here. My guardians speak highly of you.” “Then I must earn the honor anew,” Rafael replied gently, bowing his head with genuine respect. They sat, and the conversation that followed unfolded with the slow, deliberate grace of two minds that approached one another not through flirtation but through a mutual, instinctive seriousness. Rafael spoke of architecture though never boastfully describing the way Dutch homes were constructed with narrow façades yet deep foundations, how the weight of each floor demanded a delicate balance of craft and trust in the materials, and how every design required the architect to understand not only the building but the soul of the people who would inhabit it. Regina listened with a concentration that surprised him. Her questions were subtle yet perceptive: she asked how a structure could carry the memory of its builders, how light could be guided through a narrow space, how foundations were strengthened against storms and shifting earth. Rafael realized, with a quiet and unexpected stir of admiration, that she was not listening as a woman making polite conversation but as someone who understood the metaphor behind his craft. Their exchange deepened. She asked about Portugal in a tone that hinted at familiarity yet carried a shadow that Rafael recognized instinctively. He answered with restraint, describing the beauty of the land without speaking of the danger that had driven them both away, sensing that she carried memories that could not yet bear the weight of words. At one point she set the teapot down with a careful motion, and he noticed a faint tremor in her hand so slight that only a man trained to read delicate inflections would have observed it. It was not fear of him, but an involuntary echo of some past violent moment that lay dormant in her. Rafael felt no impulse to question it; rather, a deep, silent respect rose within him, the kind one feels in the presence of a fragile object repaired with invisible seams. Throughout the visit, Mrs. Brinkmeyer watched them both with the quiet, measured satisfaction of a woman who had seen many encounters and could discern the rare ones where two lives did not repel each other but rather settled into a kind of tentative, balanced orbit. She knew better than interfering. She allowed the silences to remain unbroken, trusting that these two Portuguese souls one wounded, one seeking might recognize in each other not rescue, not salvation, but the possibility of companionship grounded in dignity. When Rafael rose to leave, the light outside had grown dim, casting the canal in soft shades of blue and gold. Regina walked him to the door, not out of custom alone but out of a gentle, unspoken courtesy. As he stepped across the threshold, she spoke in a tone barely above a whisper. "Senhor Toledano... you spoke of foundations today. Of how they must be steady, even when the earth shifts. I... I appreciated that." Rafael met her gaze with quiet solemnity. "Foundations must be strengthened carefully, senhora. Sometimes slowly. And always with patience." For the first time, she allowed herself a small smile faint, fleeting, but real. When the door closed behind him, Regina stood motionless for a long moment, her fingers lingering on the polished brass of the handle. She did not yet understand what had stirred within her during the conversation, nor what faint warmth had settled across her chest like a morning sun attempting to break through a long-clouded sky. But she knew this much: Rafael Toledano had not spoken to her as a man evaluating a future bride. He had spoken to her as someone recognizing an equal mind, a soul shaped by exile, and a life not to be pitied but to be understood. As for Rafael, he walked along the canal with unhurried steps, his thoughts steady, his expression calm. Yet beneath the composure, he felt the rare, unmistakable sensation that he had just encountered someone whose presence would not leave him unchanged. He did not imagine love not yet perhaps not even soon. But he felt something deeper, something more certain, a quiet conviction formed not of passion but of respect: that fate, with all its cruel meanderings, might have finally brought him before a woman whose life echoed his own in a way he had never expected. And though neither of them could fully articulate it, the meeting had set in motion a transformation as inevitable as the turning of the tides. A transformation that would, in time, join two exiles into one story.

CHAPTER 13 THE WEDDING AT THE ESNOGA

The morning of the wedding rose over Amsterdam with solemnity that seemed drawn from the depths of the earth rather than from the sky. The autumn light was pale and finely sifted, lying gently upon the façades of the canal houses as though unwilling to disturb the city's Sabbath-like calm. Even the water in the Herengracht seemed to move with deliberate restraint, carrying its reflections with the dignity of a procession. Within this stillness, however, the Portuguese community pulsed with a quiet expectancy, for the marriage of Rafael Enríquez Diego Toledano to Regina Haya Brinkmeyer once the unknown maid Rebeca Vadias had awakened a kind of collective emotion that touched not only those who knew their stories but also those who merely sensed that something rare and luminous was about to unfold. For the wedding was not merely a union of two young lives; it was an affirmation of survival, a victory over the shadows of Lisbon and the tribunals of the Inquisition. The very act of marrying openly, in full Jewish dignity, beneath the high vaulted ceiling of the Esnoga, carried the weight of generations who had muttered blessings behind shuttered windows and who had walked through life with fear pressed against their ribs like an invisible blade. The Portuguese Synagogue, newly built and resplendent in its austere grandeur, stood that morning like a monument carved from light itself. Its vast interior, constructed without pillars so that the space might remain unobstructed for prayer, breathed with an airy solemnity that made every footstep sound like an invocation. As guests entered, their murmured greetings were swallowed by the cavernous silence, punctuated only by the soft rustle of fine garments and the muted clicking of men's shoes against the polished wooden f loor. Brass chandeliers hung in great circles overhead, unlit for the daytime ceremony yet gleaming with the promise of future

Sabbaths. Regina arrived early with Mrs. Brinkmeyer, her dress a masterpiece of understated Sephardic elegance ivory silk with narrow sleeves, modest lace at the throat, and a veil so delicate it seemed woven not from thread but from breath itself. She moved with the poised timidity of one who had learned to walk carefully through life, as though each step required a negotiation between the present and the buried remnants of her past. Her face, beneath the veil, carried a calm that was not without tremor; her eyes held the unmistakable radiance of a woman who had tasted bitterness but refused to let it define her. Rafael stood near the bimah, speaking quietly with the rabbi, his posture marked by the grave composure that had first drawn him to Regina. His suit was dark, impeccably cut, and entirely devoid of the flamboyance some young men adopted on such occasions. He stood not as a triumphant bridegroom but as a man deeply aware of the responsibility that marriage represented not only to his future wife, but to the lineage they both carried from lands that had forgotten their loyalty and punished their devotion. When the ceremony began, the Esnoga was filled with a hush so profound it felt as though the walls themselves were listening. Regina stepped toward the chuppah with small, steady steps, guided by Mrs. Brinkmeyer and accompanied by the soft murmur of blessings from the women surrounding her. Rafael watched her approach with a quiet intensity, his expression neither jubilant nor nervous, but deeply, reverently moved. Underneath the canopy the open sky's symbolic embrace rabbinic words flowed with the cadence of centuries. The blessings unfolded in long, melodic Hebrew, echoing through the vast hall with a resonance that seemed to vibrate in the very air. Those gathered felt themselves not merely witnesses to a marriage but to the reweaving of a life torn apart by exile. The Brinkmeyer's, standing among the elders of the community, held hands with the fragile pride of parents who had sheltered a wounded soul long enough to see her rise again. It was in the moment when the rabbi lifted the cup of wine to recite the blessing over the sanctification of marriage that it happened. A voice thin, trembling, rising from the far end of the synagogue's great entrance pierced the stillness with a cry so raw, so unfiltered by decorum or hesitation, that every head turned as though drawn by an invisible force. “Regina! Regina Nunez Vas!” The name her true name, her buried name, the name she had not spoken aloud in years hung in the air like a blow. For a heartbeat, the entire synagogue seemed to freeze. The rabbi’s hands stopped mid-gesture. Rafael’s breath halted. Regina felt her spine turn to iron beneath her silk dress; a tremor passed through her like a cold wind seeping under a door. Then the doors at the back of the synagogue swung open with a force that seemed almost supernatural. A young woman disheveled, thin, her hair tangled and streaked with travel-dust, her dress plain and ill-fitting stood framed in the open doorway, her chest rising and falling with ragged breaths. Her face bore the unmistakable softness of simplicity, but her eyes wide, fragile, luminous held a single blazing certainty: recognition. “Regina!” she cried again, stumbling forward, her voice breaking on the final syllable. “Regina… minha irmã…” My sister. Regina’s breath vanished. The world swayed. A murmur rippled through the congregation like distant thunder. Some guests stepped back in confusion; others leaned forward with apprehension, sensing that whatever was unfolding was no ordinary disruption but the eruption of a past too powerful to remain silent any longer. Hanna. The child she had left behind in Portugal; the sister whose fragile mind had moved like a bird fluttering between innocence and fear; the one she had imagined lost, captured, hidden, or dead. And now here she was, alive, trembling, her entire being stretched toward Regina with a desperate, instinctive certainty. Regina took one step forward, her hand rising to her veil as if to steady herself, and for a moment it seemed she might faint. But something deep within her some core forged from suffering and resilience held her upright. She walked slowly at first, then with growing urgency, toward Hanna, her veil trailing behind her like a sheet of light. Hanna saw her movement and ran awkwardly, stumbling over her own feet, tears streaking down her face. She collided with Regina in an embrace so fierce it drew gasps from those nearest. Regina wrapped her arms around her sister, lowering her face into Hanna's tangled hair, and for a long moment they stood immobile, weeping silently, the synagogue hushed around them in awe. Mrs. Brinkmeyer approached with trembling composure. She laid a hand upon Hanna's shoulder and whispered something soft, something only a mother could say to a child in distress. Hanna turned toward her with confusion, then back to Regina, clinging to her as though afraid she might vanish again. When the two sisters finally lifted their faces, the rabbi descended from the bimah, his expression grave yet tender. He looked not at the disruption but at the miracle it represented a family torn by exile reuniting before the assembly of Israel, in the very house where fear had once been forbidden to enter. Rafael approached, slowly, carefully. He did not speak; he only bowed his head slightly toward Hanna in acknowledgment, then toward Regina with the quiet certainty of a man who understood that life, in its cruelties and mercies, had intertwined his fate with hers far more deeply than marriage alone could signify. At last, The Brinkmeyer's, overcome with emotion, stepped forward, embracing Hanna with the open-hearted generosity that had saved Regina years before. Mrs. Brinkmeyer whispered gently, "You, too, are our daughter," and Hanna let out a broken sob, collapsing into her arms with the relief of a child who had finally reached home. The rabbi raised his hands again not to command silence, for silence already reigned, but to restore the sanctity of the moment. He did not rebuke; he did not admonish. He said only: "Blessed is He who restores the lost and gathers the scattered of His people." The ceremony resumed but it was no longer the same ceremony. It had transformed, acquiring a depth and gravity beyond ritual. When Rafael placed the ring upon Regina's finger, she did not stand alone beneath the chuppah; Hanna stood beside her, trembling, clutching Regina's hand as if anchored to the very center of her world. And when Rafael broke the glass in remembrance of the destroyed Temple, the congregation felt as few ever do that they had witnessed not only the shattering of loss but the triumph of reunion. For in that moment, amid the crystalline shards, the cries of the sisters, and the solemn murmuring of ancient blessings, the Nunez Vas lineage once nearly extinguished was reborn.

CHAPTER 14 LEGACY AND LIGHT

Amsterdam did not change its face the morning after the wedding, yet for the small circle of lives touched by the events beneath the sweeping roof of the Esnoga, the city had acquired a new and deeper resonance. The canals continued their slow, deliberate passage toward the sea; merchants still unrolled carpets onto the street front; women still bargained for fish in hoarse voices at the docks; and yet, beneath the surface of ordinary noise, something had quietly rearranged itself in the hearts of the Brinkmeyer household and in the young couple who now shared a future. The return of Hanna unexpected, improbable, almost biblical in its timing had become, within hours, a whispered marvel among the Sephardic families of Amsterdam. Some spoke of providence, others of coincidence, but those who had stood in the Esnoga and seen Regina's face at the moment her sister cried her name knew that what they had witnessed lay beyond the reach of simple explanation. They spoke of the fragility of exile, of the unexpected mercy that sometimes breaks into lives long accustomed to sorrow, and of the peculiar fate of two sisters who had been scattered across a continent only to be reunited on the day one of them reclaimed her name before the entire community. For Regina, the days following her marriage unfolded with an unfamiliar sense of spaciousness. She had lived for so long with fear edging every breath, fear of discovery, fear of memory, fear of the unknown that the sudden arrival of moments untouched by dread felt like a kind of bewilderment. Rafael, with his instinctive moral patience and his quiet attentiveness, understood the delicacy of this transition more intuitively than words could express. He did not urge her into cheerfulness nor demand from her the exuberance newly married couples were expected to display. Instead, he allowed silence to have its rightful place; he treated her history not as a wound to be inspected but as a mystery to be honored.

Their home, a tall and slender canal house on the Amstel, soon filled with small evidence of their combined lives. Rafael's architectural sketches lay rolled upon a desk near the window; Regina's weaving frame occupied a modest corner of the sitting room, where the steady rhythmic shuttle of thread created a sound more comforting than any music. On Friday afternoons the scent of freshly polished silver mingled with the warm fragrance of Freshly backed challah bread and other Shabbat delicacies, drifting from the kitchen up the narrow staircase and into the rafters. On the table, Regina placed the beautiful silver candlesticks her husband had bought her for her wedding, now polished and burning openly with tall, unwavering flames. For the first time since her childhood, she lit them without fear. Hanna, still overwhelmed by the forces that had carried her through Portugal and across the endless miles that separated her from her sister, lived at first in a state of soft bewilderment. She moved through the Brinkmeyer house like a fragile bird adjusting to a new cage not imprisoned, but uncertain of the boundaries of safety. Mrs. Brinkmeyer tended to her with a maternal vigilance sharpened by years of childlessness; she spoke gently, fed her patiently, and let her sleep countless hours without disturbance. When Hanna awoke, she clutched her new "mom's" hand with the same instinctive certainty she had shown in the Esnoga, as though her sister's presence was the only fixed point in a world that had for too long spun without mercy. Yet even in Hanna's simplicity, there emerged a surprising resilience. She delighted in the simple rhythms of the household; she learned the sounds of the canal boats, the patterns of the bells that signaled the hours, the whisper of the wind through the narrow alleyways. Sometimes she hummed faint melodies from their childhood songs their mother had once sung in hushed tones on Shabbat afternoons in Portugal and the notes, though halting, wove themselves through the house like a gentle blessing rediscovered. As weeks turned into months, the Brinkmeyer home and the Toledano home became, in practice, one extended household. Mr. Brinkmeyer, whose temperament favored quiet observation rather than overt declaration, watched Hanna with a tenderness he rarely expressed aloud. He saw in her the embodiment of a path fate had nearly closed and, in her reunion with Regina, the triumph of endurance over the cruelty of history. When she smiled, he felt a warmth he had thought forever denied to him. When Regina and Rafael visited, he received them with solemn pride, as though witnessing the unmistakable fruit of years he and his wife had sown with such careful love. It was in this period of calm that Regina began to recover parts of herself she had long buried. She returned to music, an art she had abandoned during her years of wandering. The harp like she had at home. The instrument stood in the corner of her home, abandoned by the previous owner of the home, its polished wood glowing in the morning light. She touched it at first with hesitance, the way one greets an old friend one has wronged by absence. But soon her fingers remembered: the delicacy of the strings, the tremulous vibration that surged from the core of the instrument into the air like a breath released from captivity. When she played, Rafael would sit in the chair by the window, listening with the attentive reverence of a soul who had found his counterpart not simply in the woman he married but in the music that carried her story. That story, once disfigured by fear and violence, now unfolded in a new rhythm one shaped by the dignity of a husband who sought not to erase her past but to illuminate the strength woven through it, the compassion of adoptive parents who had nurtured her with steadfast devotion, and the fragile innocence of a sister whose simple presence had become the living seal on Regina's deliverance. But it was not only Regina who transformed. Rafael too found himself quietly altered by the woman he had taken as his wife. Her capacity to endure sorrow without allowing bitterness to eclipse her gentleness awakened in him a humility he had never fully understood until he witnessed it embodied. He learned to measure his work not merely by the precision of his architectural lines but by the moral steadiness required to build a home worthy of the courage Regina had carried through the most harrowing trials. He slowed his pace, deepened his faith, and, in the quiet company of his wife and her sister, discovered a form of contentment that did not depend on success or recognition but on the intimate knowledge that he had become part of a redemption larger than his own life. Amsterdam, for all its bustling commerce and relentless industry, seemed to cradle their home in an unspoken covenant. The city that had received them as exiles now watched them rebuild their lives piece by fragile piece. Jewish children played in the courtyards of the community school; elderly refugees sat on benches by the canal whispering prayers in a mixture of Portuguese, Hebrew, and Dutch; carpenters, merchants, and scholars greeted each other with the familiarity of people who understood themselves to be survivors of the same long night. In this environment, Regina's family flourished. Hanna, under the gentle care of the Brinkmeyer's and the stability of routine, regained a certain measure of clarity. She would never possess the complex reasoning of an adult, yet she moved through the world with an innocent joy that softened even the hardest corners of daily life. She helped set the table on Shabbat, polishing the spoons with dutiful concentration, and would sometimes fall asleep in the early evening with her head resting on her new "mom's " lap, murmuring childhood phrases in the soft Portuguese of their mother's tung. Regina, watching her sister breathe in peaceful rhythms, felt something she had once believed forever lost: the sense that her family fractured, scattered, nearly extinguished had been restored to her, if not in its original form, then in a new one shaped by mercy. As years passed, the couple's home became known for its music, its hospitality, and the unmistakable warmth that emanated from its chambers. Rafael's architectural reputation continued to grow, but he measured his success less by commissions than by the quiet evenings he spent with his wife and her sister, by the flicker of Shabbat candles reflected in the windowpanes, by the gentle laughter that sometimes rose from the kitchen as Mrs. Brinkmeyer taught Hanna how to knead dough for the Sabbath bread. No one in Amsterdam forgot the wedding at the Esnoga the cry that had shattered the ceremony, the tears that had flowed like wine, the miracle that had appeared in the doorway of the synagogue like a living proof of divine compassion. But over time, what remained most vivid in the community's memory was not the sudden drama of that moment but the steadfast love that followed: the unhesitating embrace of the Brinkmeyer's, the patient devotion of Rafael, the dignified renewal of Regina, and the quiet happiness of Hanna. In the end, the Nunez Vas lineage once threatened with extinction did not merely survive. It flourished. It took root in Dutch soil without losing its Iberian soul. It built homes, raised children, preserved melodies and prayers, torah study, and a bait Neaman were halacha and mitzvoth were observed to the woven cloth and crafted books. And through the long winters and the fleeting summers, the lights that Regina kindled each Shabbat became symbols not of fragility but of triumph: flames that had endured tempest and exile, and which now burned with the steady brilliance of a people returned to themselves. In those candles, reflected in the still water of the Amstel, one could see the fulfillment of a promise that had traveled across borders and through the ravages of fear a promise that no darkness, however vast, could extinguish the devotion of a heart that refused to surrender its name.

CHAPTER 15 A HOME WITH MANY DOORS

The first winter after Regina's wedding arrived quietly, as if unwilling to disturb the new household that was taking shape along the Amstel. Amsterdam, with its labyrinth of canals and its bridges that arched like ribs across the water, entered its season of frost and dim afternoon light. Yet within the walls of the Toledano home, warmth gathered slowly and steadily, not only from the hearth but from the intricate weaving of lives that had once been scattered across the terrors of Europe and now converged under one roof. The house was not grand by the standards of the wealthiest merchants, but it possessed a dignified beauty of proportion its narrow façade rising with the improbable elegance that characterized Dutch canal architecture. Rafael had chosen it not for ostentation but for its sound foundations, its abundant light, and the view it offered of boats drifting soundlessly beneath the winter sky. These qualities, he had said quietly to Regina when they signed the deed, were the makings of a home where peace could be cultivated like a perennial garden. Inside, the house soon reflected a union of two worlds. On one wall hung a tapestry woven in the sober, geometric Dutch manner; opposite it, Regina placed a piece of fine white damask linen she had woven herself, its delicate sheen a whisper of Portugal's lost gentility. In the corner, Rafael's architectural desk was arranged with precise order: drafting instruments, parchment, charcoal sticks, a Portuguese psalter, and a Tanach, Chumash resting side by side like two long-separated friends newly reacquainted. And near the hearth stood the harp that had once belonged to the previous owner of the home, its strings restored by a skilled artisan so that the instrument seemed ready to breathe music into the air again, despite years of silence. Hanna lived by the Brinkmeyer's by choice, not by necessity. Brinkmeyer's remained her guardians in the eyes of the community, she had, from the moment of the wedding, attached herself to them. She slept in a small adjoining room furnished with simple comforts:

a woolen blanket embroidered with flowers, a wooden chest for her few belongings, and a single window overlooking the canal. When she awoke each morning, it was mama she whispered, as though verifying the reality of the home she had found after so many years of wandering. Her presence brought both tenderness and challenge. At times she moved through the house with an ethereal quiet, absorbed in some private world that Mr. or Mrs. Brinkmeyer could fully enter. At other times she required guidance with the simplest tasks: tying a ribbon, separating the spices for the Sabbath meal, or remembering to dry her hands after washing. Yet even in these moments, there was no burden only the echo of a promise Regina had once made to herself: that if she ever saw her sister again, she would never allow her to be alone in the world. The community received Hanna with a mixture of compassion and respectful caution. Amsterdam, though tolerant, was still shaped by expectations of decorum, and the reintroduction of a woman whose mind had not been fully developed, bruised by exile and fear required sensitivity. Yet the Portuguese Jews, themselves refugees of unimaginable trials, understood vulnerability; they had learned that brokenness did not diminish humanity. Many greeted Hanna with gentle nods when she accompanied Regina to the market or to the synagogue. Some women even approached Regina quietly, offering advice, comfort, or simple fellowship. One elderly widow, who had lost two sons in the Inquisition's prisons, placed her hand upon Hanna's head and murmured a blessing that left Regina in tears. Rafael, for his part, adapted to Hanna's presence with a grace that astonished even Regina. He had always been patient, but with Hanna he revealed a tenderness that seemed to flow from some deep reservoir of kindness. He showed her how to recognize the chiming of the city's bell towers, how to identify the different boats along the canal, how to help in small, manageable ways without overwhelming her. Sometimes, in the evenings, Regina would watch them from the doorway: Rafael sitting at his desk, drafting a canal house, while Hanna quietly sorted his charcoal sticks by size, humming a melody that only her fragile memory retained. In those moments, Regina felt an overflowing gratitude she had no language for a sense that her life, once shattered like pottery dashed against stone, had been gathered and reassembled with hands far more merciful than fate alone would have allowed. Their home soon became known among the Sephardic families as a place of warmth and welcome. Not in the loud, extravagant sense, but through a doorway always open to travelers, students, and those who carried letters from Lisbon, Porto, or Seville. Many evenings found Rafael debating philosophy or torah, gemara, or Rambam with young scholars, while Regina served spiced tea and listened with quiet interest. Mothers brought their daughters to learn weaving or the melodies of old Portuguese hymns from her; merchants came to seek Rafael's advice on house expansions or warehouse designs. The house developed a reputation not simply as the dwelling of a young couple but as a meeting place where the past and future of the community intertwined. Shabbat transformed the house into a sanctuary of luminous calm. Regina lit the candles with the devotion of a woman who had once lit them in darkness and fear; now their flames rose with unfettered brightness, casting a golden glow across the polished table. Rafael received the Sabbath with a voice that carried both Iberian depth and Dutch clarity, his chanting weaving itself through the rooms like a gentle tide. Hanna, seated beside Regina, often watched the flames with wide, wondering eyes, sometimes reaching out her hand to the halo of warmth that emanated from them, as though confirming that the light truly belonged to them now. In these moments, Regina felt the full weight and wonder of her new existence: she was no longer the hunted girl fleeing Portugal under a false name, nor the servant hiding in the shadows of Amsterdam's merchant houses. She was mistress of her own home, wife to a man who honored her, sister to a woman restored to her arms, and daughter of two parents who though far away might yet still walk the earth. She lived not only with memory but with hope. The household continued to grow, not only in affection but in purpose. Rafael's influence within the community deepened as his architectural works began shaping the very face of the Jewish quarter. Regina's weaving became sought after, her damask linens prized for their meticulous craftsmanship and the almost imperceptible softness that felt like a blessing woven into thread. Hanna, too, found a small place of her own: she helped prepare Shabbat candles under Regina's guidance and became known for her pure, melodic humming an unexpected gift that calmed even the most restless visitors. Their home soon came to symbolize something quietly extraordinary: it was a refuge where no door was closed to those in need. The poorest students found meals there; the loneliest widows found company; the new arrivals from the Iberian Peninsula found counsel and warmth. Without ever seeking it, Regina became known among the women as someone who understood suffering without judgment and hope without naivety. Thus began the years that would shape the heart of Regina's adulthood. Years of growth, healing, steady joy, and quiet purpose. Years in which the threads of her life, once frayed and scattered, were gathered into a tapestry rich with meaning and light. What Regina could not know not yet, not even in her most hopeful dreams was that the walls of her home, so newly warmed by the presence of her sister and her husband, would soon witness a miracle she had long believed impossible: the return of the two faces she had thought lost to history forever.

CHAPTER 16 CHILDREN OF TWO LANDS

Spring in Amsterdam arrived not with the sudden exuberance of southern lands but with a slow, steady unveiling, as if the city so accustomed to restraint preferred to open itself to warmth incrementally. The canals thawed one thin layer at a time, releasing glints of reflected sunlight that shimmered across the water like broken glass turned to gold. The plane trees lining the narrow streets unfurled their buds carefully, as though testing the air before committing themselves to the season. And into this hesitant awakening came the first quiet signs that the Toledano household was, in its own way, preparing for a rebirth. Regina discovered she was with child in early Nissan, when she found herself pausing more frequently during her morning tasks, one hand instinctively moving toward her abdomen as if acknowledging a presence before she could articulate it. She told Rafael in the soft, breathless manner of a woman who wonders if speaking too loudly might disturb the fragile miracle she carries. His reaction, though restrained by temperament, radiated an unmistakable joy; he cupped her face gently between his hands, not with triumph but with awe, as though he were touching the threshold of something sacred. From that moment forward, the house shifted. Not dramatically nothing in Regina and Rafael's world ever altered in sudden, violent strokes but in subtle, cumulative ways that revealed a new center of gravity forming within their walls. Hanna, who understood the news not intellectually but in the instinctive, emotional language that governed her life, clung to Regina with renewed protectiveness. She often laid her ear against Regina's belly, whispering in Portuguese the half-remembered lullabies she had once heard their mother sing. Regina would stroke her hair, feeling an ache that was equal parts memory and yearning, imagining a future where her children might inherit something gentler than the fear she and Hanna had known. The community, too, responded with a warmth that bordered on reverence. Women visited with advice, herbs, and stories of their own pregnancies; elderly men nodded to Rafael with the approving gravity reserved for a young father-to-be. Even the rabbi normally composed in scholarly detachment allowed himself an uncharacteristic smile when he blessed the couple one Shabbat evening, murmuring that their home would soon be "filled with the laughter of generations that Portugal tried but failed to extinguish." The pregnancy unfolded with the quiet serenity that had become the signature of Regina's life in Amsterdam. She moved slowly now, not from weakness but from deliberate intention, as though savoring each moment of the unfolding future. She continued to weave, though her threads grew softer, her patterns more intimate linens for swaddling, cloth that bore the delicate faint sheen of motherly anticipation. Rafael worked at his architectural plans with new resolve, sketching designs for homes that would one day shelter families as tightly knit as his own. And then, on an early summer morning when the canal reflected the sky in a pale wash of blue, their first child was born a son. His arrival was not dramatic; there were no storms, no cries beyond the ordinary pain of labor, no omens etched across the heavens. But when Regina held him for the first time tiny, warm, fragile, yet radiating the fierce vulnerability of new life she felt a sensation she had not known since childhood: a complete and unbroken sense of belonging. The child bore her father's eyes and Rafael's serene brow; his tiny fists curled with the quiet determination of a survivor's descendant. They named him Benjamin Nunez Toledano, after Rafael's father and Regina's family line, uniting the Portuguese past with their Dutch present. News traveled quickly. The Brinkmeyer's arrived within hours, Mrs. Brinkmeyer weeping freely as she held the infant, whispering blessings in a mixture of Dutch and Portuguese. Hanna hovered nearby, uncertain whether she dared to touch him, until Regina guided her hands gently to the baby's warm bundle. Hanna giggled a bright, clear sound rarely heard since childhood and declared in her simple, earnest way that she would protect him always. In the months that followed, Regina and Rafael watched their son grow with a mixture of vigilance and wonder. His f irst laugh brought Rafael to tears; his first steps unsteady and brave left Regina standing motionless for minutes afterward, overwhelmed by the sight of a child living freely on land where she had once fled for her life. And as he grew, so too did their family. A daughter followed two years later, named Miriam after Rafael's mother; then another son, Solomon, in honor of Regina's lost brother whose memory lingered in her heart like a fading but sacred melody. Each child carried a different blend of their heritage. Benjamin possessed Rafael's introspective calm and Regina's intuitive sensitivity. Miriam inherited her grandmother's quiet authority; she watched the world with solemn curiosity, as though absorbing its patterns before choosing how to respond. Solomon, born with a gentle disposition and a smile that came easily, reminded Regina so strongly of her brother that she often found herself whispering prayers of gratitude and grief in the same breath. The Toledano household grew in sound as well as number. The once-silent rooms now rang with the patter of small feet, the laughter of children chasing each other through narrow staircases, the playful hum of Hanna joining their games with childlike enthusiasm. Rafael built a cradle by hand; Regina filled it with linens woven from threads imbued with her own memories, each cloth a testament to the transformation of a life once marked by loss. Yet beneath this tapestry of domestic joy ran a deeper, more complex current: the blending of two lands, two identities, two histories. Regina taught her children Portuguese lullabies and Hebrew prayers; Rafael taught them Dutch manners and the craft of careful observation. They grew up speaking three languages Portuguese in affection, Dutch in daily matters, Hebrew in devotion. Their lives were not divided by this multiplicity; rather, they were enriched by it, as though they carried within them an entire continent's worth of resilience and culture. Amsterdam, for its part, shifted too. The Jewish community flourished, enriched by the arrival of new refugees fleeing Iberian oppression. Merchants prospered; scholars wrote; musicians composed melodies that blended the mournful sighs of the Portuguese fado with the lively tempo of Dutch folk rhythms. And throughout these changes, the Toledano children moved like small, bright threads woven into the larger tapestry of a community that understood exile yet lived with hope. Regina watched her children grow with a sense of wonder that bordered on astonishment. She had once believed her family was destroyed scattered by persecution, silenced by fear, extinguished like a single candle swallowed by the winds of history. Yet here, in her home, barefoot on the wooden floorboards, three new lives danced with unburdened joy. They were not haunted by the shadows of Portugal; they belonged wholly to the land that had given them refuge and life. But even as she gathered her family around the Shabbat table, lit candles that flickered with sacred constancy, and sang melodies that blended the old world with the new, a quiet yearning stirred within her. A question she had tried not to ask for years, yet which returned with persistent, silent gravity: Were her parents still alive? She had seen Hanna restored. She had seen her lineage renewed. She had seen miracles unfold with the solemn grandeur of providence. But one absence remained. One silence. One wound. And though she hid it beneath the blessings she whispered over her children each Friday evening, the longing did not fade. If anything, it deepened sharpened by the awareness that her family's story, though profoundly renewed, remained incomplete. The answer to that ache was already moving toward her across roads and borders, carried by the footsteps of someone who had seen what she feared to hope. The secret traveler was coming.

CHAPTER 17 THE PLAGUE YEARS

There are years in a city's life that pass quietly, like pages turned in a book read in good light, the words flowing smoothly, the story advancing with neither shock nor rupture, only the gentle accumulation of days. And then there are years when the pages seem to darken, when the ink itself grows heavy, and every line is marked by the tension between breath and its possible absence. For Amsterdam, one such year arrived when Regina's eldest, Benjamin, had just turned eight, when Miriam was five and solemn, and little Solomon still clung to his mother's skirts whenever the world grew too loud. It began with whispers, as such things always do: a rumor of illness in a distant quarter of the city, a ship docked with too many men carried out on stretchers, a woman seen weeping in the street with her shawl drawn over her head in a way that spoke not of ordinary grief but of a kind of stunned, uncomprehending terror. People shook their heads and said it was nothing, a fever passing through the poorer neighborhoods as it did every few seasons. But the whispers thickened, multiplied, and began to coil themselves around names, streets, entire families. Soon it was no longer "a fever" but the fever, and then strangers began calling it by the name everyone feared, and no one wanted to speak aloud: plague. For those who had lived through other forms of catastrophe Inquisition, exile, the slow strangulation of religious persecution the specter of plague felt both familiar and different. Familiar in that it was once again a force that could not be reasoned with, bribed, argued away, or softened by promises; different in that it was utterly indiscriminate. The Inquisition had chosen its victims with cruel, deliberate intent. The plague chose blindly, answering to no bishop, no tribunal, no doctrine only to its own obscure and merciless laws. In the Jewish quarter, where memory was already shaped by a history of being singled out and blamed, old fears stirred like dust shaken from long-closed garments. Men who had once watched their parents dragged before tribunals in Lisbon now watched the gathering of city cartmen and wondered whether, if the dead were too numerous, the blame would once again fall on their people this time accused of sorcery, poison, invisible curses. And yet Amsterdam was not Lisbon, and the Dutch authorities, for all their flaws, did not wear the face of the Inquisition. Still, fear does not consult reason before lodging itself in a person's chest. In the Toledano household, the plague's approach was f irst felt not as a physical presence but as a shifting in atmosphere an invisible tightening of the world beyond their door. The children were told to avoid crowded markets; play in the street was forbidden. Rafael began washing his hands with ritual precision not merely before prayers but after each visit to a merchant house or construction site. Regina, who had once walked the city with a survivalist's quiet vigilance, now watched for different dangers: the pallor on a neighbor's face, the too-quick burial of a man whose name she had heard only days earlier, the growing number of houses where the shutters remained closed all day. One evening, when the sun had sunk behind the silhouette of the gabled roofs and the canal reflected the sky's last smoldering colors, Regina stood at the window, watching the slow passage of a narrow boat carrying two city wardens and a physician marked by a feather in his hat. They stopped at a house two streets away. A bundle no larger than a child was carried out and laid on the planks. Hanna, who had been humming softly as she sorted clean linen, fell silent, her eyes fixed on the scene with an almost animal wariness. Regina reached for her hand, and they stood together, a silence between them that did not need words. That night, after the children had been put to bed and the house had settled into its nocturnal hush, Regina and Rafael sat at the table across from one another, a single candle burning between them. The flame cast slow shifting shadows upon their faces, marking every line of care and every contour of resolve. "We have known danger before," Rafael said quietly, as if reminding himself as much as her. "We survived Portugal. We survived the escape. We have built a home here. We will not abandon our trust now." Regina nodded, though her hands remained folded tightly in her lap. "Trust," she echoed.

"Not in the city. Not in physicians. In the One who decides who breathes and who does not." Only decided by Hashem our Father. He looked at her with the gravity that had first drawn her to him. "Yes. In Him. But He did not give us sense and responsibility so that we might throw them aside and call it faith. We will be careful. We will protect the children, and Hanna, and your parents if..." He paused, realizing he had spoken a thought that did not yet belong to this moment. "We will protect those entrusted to us." The days that followed unfolded with a strange duality: on the surface, life continued bread was baked, lessons were taught, clothes were mended but beneath everything ran the steady drumbeat of mortality's proximity. The synagogue remained open, but prayers grew heavier, each word uttered with the urgency of those who knew they might not have many such opportunities left. Names were read for recovery; candles were lit for the dead. The community's charitable funds were strained by the growing number of widows and orphans. Regina found herself moving between two states: an almost mechanical focus on tasks and an inward attentiveness sharp as a blade. She refused to let fear rule her, yet she knew better than to dismiss it entirely. She remembered what terror could do to a person's mind, how it could hollow out the will and leave behind only the instinct to flee or hide. She had spent too many years living like that; she would not let her children inherit such a posture toward the world. Instead, she chose a different response: vigilance without panic, prayer without despair. She boiled water for washing; she scrubbed the entrance f loor more often; she burned lavender and rosemary in small dishes, following the advice of women aged enough to have lived through lesser epidemics. She kept the children close, turning their confinement into a kind of game. Stories were told at length. Psalms were recited together, not as gloomy incantations but as familiar songs whose rhythms anchored the heart. For Hanna, the plague awakened buried echoes of old fear. She had vague but piercing memories of Portugal people whispering in corners, sudden disappearances, the constant sense that something unnamed might happen at any moment. She began to ask, in her halting way, whether "the bad men" would come again, whether they would take Regina, whether the boats on the canal carried judges. Regina held her face in both hands and spoke with steady tenderness. "No, minha Hanna. This is not like before. The danger now is not men with anger in their eyes but a sickness that no one can see. We will be careful. We will stay together. No one will take you from me again." Her words, though simple, were built on the solid ground of a promise long forged in the fire of their shared past. Hanna believed her, because she needed to, and because Regina had never once betrayed that trust. The children, in their own way, absorbed the gravity of the time without fully comprehending its implications. Benjamin, with his father's thoughtful nature, observed the changing patterns of the street and asked questions about why some houses suddenly displayed white flags or why certain doors received no visitors. Miriam watched her mother closely, imitating her calm; when she sensed Regina's unease, she took it upon herself to distract Solomon with games and stories. Solomon, still young enough to drift easily between fear and play, clung often to his mother's dress, as if her physical nearness were a protective talisman. As the number of sick increased, the community organized itself with the efficiency of those who understood mutual responsibility as a commandment, not a choice. Men volunteered to bury the dead when Christian gravediggers refused to handle Jewish bodies. Women prepared food for households where illness had struck. Those who were physically strong took on the risk of bringing supplies to quarantined homes. Rafael, despite Regina's unspoken dread at the thought of him exposing himself, joined a small group tasked with coordinating such efforts, the biggest mitzva known to mankind Chessed Shel Emeth to do Chessed, that the receivers, cant thank you for. his natural sense of order turning the chaotic needs of the neighborhood into manageable lists and routes. One evening, after he had returned later than usual, his coat smelling faintly of smoke and lye, he sat heavily in his chair and ran a hand across his face. Regina set a bowl of hot soup before him and noticed a tremor she had rarely seen in him. "Today," he said, after a long pause, "we buried a boy not much older than Benjamin." The words hung between them like a cold stone. "He had been studying to be a sofer," Rafael continued, "a scribe. His hands looked as though they had been made for letters. His father placed his inkwell in the grave with him." He swallowed, his throat tight. "His mother did not cry. She only stood there, holding her shawl, as if... as if grief had frozen in her." Regina reached across the table and placed her hand over his. "You are doing a mitzvah," she said softly. "Not everyone is asked to face death so directly. It is not a punishment. It is a burden entrusted." He nodded, but his eyes were shadowed. "I keep thinking," he admitted, "what if one of ours " She did not let him finish. "We will not live in that thought," she said firmly. "We know it is possible. We do not deny it. But we will not feed it." He looked at her, and in that gaze there was the silent recognition that her strength, once nearly crushed by exile and assault, had grown into something formidable: a gentleness that did not bend before fear. In the synagogue, the rabbi spoke often of the balance between hishtadlut human effort and bitachon trust in God. Some men came with eyes flashing, demanding an explanation for why the righteous were falling sick alongside the indifferent. Others came with shoulders bowed, speaking in low voices of children lost, asking whether they had failed in some hidden way. To all of them he said, in varying forms, that human beings were not accountants of Heaven's mysteries; they were custodians of their own choices. Their task was not to decipher why each blow fell where it did, but to respond with as much compassion and steadfastness as they could muster. Regina drank in these words, for they resonated with the path she had chosen since her arrival in Amsterdam. She could not control what the world did or what disease did but she could control whether her home remained a place of refuge or became a fortress of panic. And so, as the city counted its dead and the plague continued its slow, pitiless march through alleys and across bridges, the Toledano house became, even more than before, a home with many doors. They did not fling them open recklessly; they did not invite contagion.

But to those in desperate need a widow whose husband had just been buried, a child who had lost his parents and wandered sobbing through the Jewish streets, an old man with no one to cook him a meal Regina and Rafael offered what they could: a bowl of soup, a bed for a night, a corner of their table, a prayer said together with trembling lips. In those months, their children learned something no lesson could have taught them: that fear and kindness could coexist; that danger did not cancel their obligation to one another; that the fragility of life was not an argument against love but its most urgent justification. The plague did not pass quickly. It lingered, as sorrow does, receding only to surge again in new streets. But slowly, gradually, the number of new graves lessened. The harsh ringing of the city bell that had marked large death tolls grew less frequent. Shutters opened more often. Boats returned to their usual traffic. The city exhaled, cautiously. When the worst had passed, the community emerged altered not only thinned by loss but thickened by the memory of shared endurance. New orphans had to be housed, new widows supported, new questions answered. The fabric of communal life had been stretched, but it had not torn. In the Toledano home, all three children survived. Hanna, too, remained untouched by the sickness, though she had spent many sleepless nights sitting on the floor of Regina's room, clutching her sister's hand, murmuring in her half-formed language that she was afraid the shadows from Portugal had followed them. Regina would stroke her hair and answer the same each time: "No, minha Hanna. That chapter is closed. This danger is different. And it is passing." Yet something else happened in those years of fear: Regina's quiet longing for her parents, once buried beneath the urgency of daily life, had grown sharper. The plague reminded her that time was not an endless road but a finite path whose length no one could see in advance. Each death, each funeral, each name read in the synagogue's mournful cadence stirred the question anew: if her parents still lived, how many years remained to find them? And if they were gone, would she ever know, or would she live out her days with that uncertainty lodged in her like an unhealed splinter? She remained, outwardly, the same: calm, attentive, devoted to her children, her husband, her sister, and her adopted parents. But Rafael, who had long ago learned to read the fine script beneath her silences, knew that the plague had not only brushed past their home physically; it had touched something in her soul. It had reminded her, with ruthless clarity, that not all separations are eternal but some become so if too much time is allowed to pass. It was in the first relatively calm spring after the plague years that the door of the Toledano house opened one afternoon to admit a man whose presence would change everything. He was not remarkable at first glance lean from travel, his cloak dusty, his beard streaked with gray but his eyes carried the weary alertness of one accustomed to crossing borders not only of geography but of danger. He introduced himself as a traveler from Antwerp, bearing news from Lisbon, Porto, and beyond. Regina, hearing the word Lisbon, felt the room tilt for a moment. The air seemed to thicken, and the voices around her receded into a distant murmur. The plague had reminded her that life could change overnight. She did not yet know that this man, with his worn boots and cautious speech, had come to deliver not death, but the first clear sign that the past she had left behind in fear was not finished with her. Nor she with it. The secret he carried had traversed oceans of time and peril. Her parents, long buried in her heart among the dead, were not in the grave after all. They were moving toward her, one step, one message, one prayer at a time. And the house that had survived exile and plague was about to receive its most unexpected guests.

CHAPTER 18 THE SECRET TRAVELER

In the weeks that followed the traveler's first visit, time seemed to fold upon itself in the Toledano house, as if the past and the present had entered into a quiet negotiation over whose claims would be honored. The letter from Évora lay in a small wooden box near Regina's bed, wrapped in the same piece of worn linen that had once shielded her mother's amulet. She had read the letter only once, slowly, tracing each line with her fingertip, stopping when the words blurred and the ink dissolved into tears, then beginning again when she felt strong enough to endure the fragile, aching intimacy of her father's hand returning to her across so many lost years. The words themselves were simple, almost austere, as though Manuel Nunez Vas feared that excess emotion would cause the parchment to catch fire. He told of the night soldiers had come to the estate and found the house empty; of the accusations that followed; of his arrest and brief imprisonment; of Raquel's desperate visits to officials and priests, bartering whatever dignity remained to her in order to secure his release; of the slow unraveling of their property, their name, their position. He wrote of Solomon in careful, measured phrases, as if each sentence had to be carried across a chasm. "Your brother," he had written, "lived as if walking through smoke, his mind never fully returning from that terrible day in the stables. He grew quieter with each passing year, but he remained gentle, devoted, incapable of anger. He spoke your name in his sleep until the very end. He died as he had lived, with innocence in his eyes and your mother's hand in his. We buried him in a place where no priest would see the stones we placed for him, and I whispered Kaddish, though my lips trembled so much that I could hardly form the words." Regina had read that passage with a numbness that only slowly gave way to pain. She did not weep for hours, but when the tears finally came, they were not brief, theatrical sobs; they were deep, silent tears that soaked the pillow long into the night, while Rafael lay beside her, awake and listening, knowing that there are griefs one cannot interrupt with comfort, only accompany with presence. He said little, but his hand never left her arm, a steady weight that anchored her to a reality in which she was not alone, even as the ghosts of Portugal crowded around her bed. The letter ended not with accusation or even with lament, but with a plea that was also a blessing. "If it is permitted," her father had written, "and if your life is safe there, and if God opens the way, we wish to come to you before our bones grow too heavy to move. We wish to see with our own eyes that you live as a Jew, not in whispers but in song. We wish to place our hands on your head and bless you before we die, as parents are commanded to do. If it cannot be, then know that our souls are already at your table every Sabbath, standing near the candles we imagine you lighting. We carry no reproach toward you, only love. You did what we begged you to do: you survived." From the moment she finished reading, her prayer changed. Until then, her daily words had been filled with gratitude for the life she had built and supplication that it might remain intact. Now she added a single, repeated plea: that Heaven grant her the time and the means to see her parents alive, not only in letters and memories, before it was too late. Elias Andrade, the traveler, did not disappear after delivering the letter. He remained in Amsterdam for several months, visiting other households, carrying messages whose content he never disclosed. When he returned to the Toledano home a second time, his presence no longer filled the room with the pure shock of Lisbon's voice entering their Dutch refuge; rather, it brought with it the tension of a question half-answered and half-owed. He sat again at their table, this time with less dust on his boots and a little more color in his face, as though the hospitality of the community had restored some of the strength that the roads had taken from him. The children watched him with awe, sensing that he was a sort of living bridge between stories and destinations. Hanna hovered in the doorway, uncertain whether to approach, her eyes wide and unblinking, as though fearing that any sudden movement might cause him to vanish and take his news with him. "I have written," he said quietly, after the first greetings and the obligatory inquiries about health, "to your parents. I have described your home, your children, your position in the community. I have told them that you are safe and honored here. And they have answered." He reached into his satchel and produced a second, thinner letter. This time the handwriting was not Manuel's careful, measured script, but a more fluid, slanted hand that seemed to move across the page like a melody. "Your mother," he said. Regina's fingers shook as she took the parchment. She did not open it immediately; instead she held it, closed, against her heart, as one might hold a relic or a long-lost relic of childhood. When at last she unfolded it, the voice that rose from the lines pierced her like a familiar song heard after decades of silence. "My child, meu coração," it began, "I have dreamt of this moment so many nights that to write these words while awake feels like walking inside a dream that has chosen not to vanish with the dawn." The letter did not dwell long on suffering; Raquel's temperament had never leaned toward indulgent lamentation. Instead, she filled the page with images of resilience: the small Sabbath lamp hidden in a clay jar in their rented room; the secret braiding of challah made from what little flour they had; the whispered Shema said into the folds of her blanket when she feared the walls might have ears. She spoke of Solomon with the tenderness of a heart that had accepted the unchangeable while refusing to let grief turn him into a symbol rather than a person. "He left this world with your name on his lips," she wrote, "and with the peace of a soul that did not know how to hate. If you ever blame yourself for not having been there, I beg you to remove that stone from your chest. You were exactly where we needed you to be: alive, somewhere in God's world, so that our line would not end with the earth falling back upon our son's coffin." At the end, she addressed the future directly. "Your father and I are old, but we are not yet finished. If the roads remain passable and the seas are kind, we will come. I do not know whether my hands will be steady enough to braid challah in your kitchen, or whether my legs will bear me from your door to your synagogue, but I know this: I will come if my heart continues to beat. Tell your children that there is an old woman in Portugal who whispers their names into her prayers before she has ever seen their faces." When Regina finished, she did not weep as violently as she had with the first letter; instead, a quiet warmth settled over her, like a shawl placed upon her shoulders. For the first time in years, she felt not only the ache of separation but the forward pull of a promised meeting. The road between Évora and Amsterdam, once a vague abstraction of danger and distance, suddenly felt like a taut line along which love itself was traveling. "How?" she asked Elias, when she had regained her voice. "How will they come? They are old. My father has been ill. My mother writes with courage, but courage cannot make bones younger." Elias inclined his head. "They cannot take the overland route alone," he said. "It would break them. But there are ships. There is a small network merchants, rabbis, a few sympathetic captains who help move those who must leave Iberia before it becomes their grave. Your parents have already been moved from their first hiding place closer to Lisbon. There is a captain I trust, a man who will not sell them for a handful of coins. If the arrangements can be made, they will travel first to Antwerp and from there by smaller boat to Amsterdam." Rafael leaned forward. "What do you require?" Elias's eyes flickered, not with greed but with the calculation of one accustomed to balancing moral urgency against material limitations. "They will need passage money," he said. "Not only for themselves, but for one other who will accompany them a relative of mine who knows the routes and the signs to watch for. They will need letters of guarantee from your rabbi and from someone of standing in the community, to reassure skeptical officials that they are not paupers who will become a burden. And they will need fervent prayer, because the sea and the roads still answer to no man." Rafael glanced at Regina, saw in her face the answer before she spoke, and nodded. "You shall have what you need," he said. "If I must sell my sketches or borrow against future work, so be it. Money can be re-earned. Parents cannot." Elias gave a small, respectful bow. "I expected nothing less from what I have seen of this house," he replied. The weeks that followed became a season of double life for Regina. Outwardly, she fulfilled her duties with the same serene diligence as before: she guided the children's learning, kept the house in order, accompanied Hanna through her small rituals of security, welcomed guests, oversaw the weaving of linens, and lit the Sabbath candles with hands that had become steadier with the years. Inwardly, however, each day carried a subtle tremor. The letters had turned hope into something more solid, more dangerous: expectation. Every knock on the door became a question. Every mention of a ship in the harbor pricked her ears. When the wind shifted and the smell of the sea grew stronger, she found her thoughts drifting not to the docks of Amsterdam but to the Atlantic waters her parents would soon cross, imagining them leaning on one another for balance, their feet unsteady upon the deck, their eyes squinting into the horizon with a mixture of dread and anticipation. She tried not to imagine all the ways in which the journey could be broken: illness on the road, betrayal by a hired guide, a sudden crackdown by local authorities; a storm at sea; the indifferent turning away of a port official. Instead, she focused on preparing herself and her home for the possibility that they might truly arrive. She opened the chest where she kept the last linens woven in Portugal and aired them near the window, allowing the Dutch light to pass through the Iberian fabric as if reconciling the two climates. now destined to stand before Raquel's eyes in a house of open worship. She sorted through the few objects she had carried from the estate the small box with its cracked lid, the pair of silver spoons, the fragment of lace from her wedding dress and arranged them upon a shelf in the front room, as though forming a small altar to memory ready to greet those who had given her life. The children were gradually initiated into the magnitude of what was coming. Benjamin, old enough to grasp the sweep of the story, listened with grave attention when Regina told him how his grandparents had smuggled Shabbat into their lives beneath the gaze of those who despised them. Miriam seemed to understand less the historical aspect and more emotional: she pressed herself against Regina's side and asked whether her

grandmother would braid her hair, whether her grandfather would tell her stories. Little Solomon, named for the uncle he would never meet, absorbed it in fragments, occasionally announcing with absolute conviction that "the old saba and savta from Portugal" were already on the water and would arrive "before the next big rain." Hanna moved between excitement and fear like a tide. On some days she repeated, almost dreamily, "Mama, Papa, Mama, Papa," as if tasting the words on her tongue after years of famine; on others she fell into a clinging anxiety, afraid that the same forces which had torn them apart once would simply repeat their cruelty. At night she sometimes woke with a muffled cry, speaking in a confused mix of Portuguese and Dutch of doors breaking open and torches in the courtyard. Each time, Regina soothed her with the same promise. "If they come, they will come to us here, where no one can take us away from one another again. And if Heaven does not allow it, then we will carry them in our hearts as we have done all these years. But we will not suffer in advance for a pain that has not yet been given to us." At last, on a cool morning that smelled of salt and coal and the faint sweetness of spring beginning to pierce the chill, Elias appeared at their door again. This time he did not remove his cloak before speaking; his urgency entered the room like a gust of wind. "They have reached Antwerp," he said. "The hardest part is over. They survived the road. The ship is in the harbor now, and they will sail north with the tide. If all goes well, they will arrive within a week, perhaps less." Regina gripped the back of a chair to steady herself. "A week," she repeated, as if testing the word for weight. "Less, perhaps," Elias said. "The winds are favorable." Rafael laid a hand upon her arm. "We will go to the harbor when ships are expected," he said gently. "We will not wait for them to be led to our door like strangers. We will be there when they step on Dutch soil." The days that followed were among the longest in Regina's life, not because nothing happened, but because everything that did seemed only preparation for what truly mattered. The rabbi wrote letters of welcome; the Brinkmeyer's sent word that they would stand beside their adopted daughter when she greeted her parents; neighbors offered practical advice about the harbor, the officials, the schedules of arriving ships. The children rehearsed what they would say, as if meeting royalty. Hanna moved through the house in an almost trancelike state, murmuring prayers under her breath, some of which Regina recognized and some of which seemed to be compositions of her own a patchwork of psalms, childhood phrases, and words of pleading. On the morning the ship was due, the sky over Amsterdam lay low and gray, not in anger but in a kind of solemn neutrality. The canal traffic had taken on its usual busy rhythm by the time Rafael and Regina left the house, accompanied by the Brinkmeyer's, the children, and Hanna, who clung to Regina's arm as fervently as a child clings to a parent on the first day of a frightening journey. Elias walked ahead, his step guided by the intimate knowledge of someone who had traced these routes many times. The harbor was a world unto itself: a forest of masts, ropes creaking in the damp air, gulls circling and screaming overhead, dockworkers shouting in Dutch, Portuguese, Spanish, and tongues Regina could not identify. The smell of tar, salt, fish, and coal mingled into a pungent veil. As they stood on the pier indicated by Elias, Regina felt her heart beating so violently she wondered if the sound might be audible above the cacophony. "That one," Elias said at last, pointing to a modest ship easing toward the quay, its hull scarred by previous voyages, its sails furled with slow deliberation. "They are on that ship." Regina's hands began to tremble. She saw them first not as individuals but as part of a small cluster of figures near the bow, their outlines blurred by distance and the shifting air between sea and shore. As the ship drew nearer, the group resolved into shapes, then into postures, then into faces. Her mother's hair, once dark with only a few silver threads, was now almost entirely white, wrapped beneath a simple kerchief. Her figure had thinned, but her back remained straighter than one might expect of a woman who had carried so much weight for so long. Her father's shoulders had stooped; his face bore new lines, etched with the sharp instrument of suffering, but his eyes oh, his eyes remained essentially unchanged: deep, searching, carrying a light that no tribunal, no jail, no hunger had been able to extinguish. Regina could not recall later whether she waited for the gangplank to be fully lowered or whether she moved before decorum allowed it. She only knew that at some point her body acted without consulting her mind. She found herself running, the hem of her skirt catching on a protruding board, her breath tearing at her lungs, Hanna stumbling beside her, the children calling out with a mixture of fear and exhilaration. "Máe!" she cried, the word bursting from her with such force that conversations on the dock stilled, heads turned, and even the gulls seemed to pause in their f light. For a heartbeat, no one responded. Then the woman at the rail jerked upright, her hand flying to her kerchief, her eyes scanning the crowd with the frantic intensity of someone who has dreamed too often of seeing a face that is never there. “Regina?” she whispered, though the distance swallowed the sound. They saw each other fully then, not as ghosts in memory or letters on fragile sheets but as present, breathing women standing on opposite sides of an expanse about to be bridged. The world did not vanish, but it receded. The harbor sounds blurred into a distant roar. The smell of salt thickened, as if the sea itself were holding its breath. The gangplank was lowered; a sailor shouted instructions; passengers began to descend. Raquel did not wait for permission. With the reckless determination of a mother who has carried grief like a stone in her chest for too many years, she moved forward, her feet uncertain on the planks but her gaze absolutely fixed. They met halfway, not on polished floors or in a sheltered room, but on rough wood smelling of brine and tar. Regina fell into her mother’s arms with a sob that seemed to come from the deepest layer of her being. Raquel held her with a strength that defied her years, one hand clutching the back of her daughter’s head as if to ensure she could not possibly slip away again. They did not speak at first; there were no words vast enough to contain what passed between them in those moments of trembling contact. When they finally drew back far enough to see each other’s faces clearly, both women laughed through their tears, a strange, stretched sound caught between disbelief and relief. “Meu Deus,” Raquel whispered, her hands framing Regina’s face as she had done when she was a child. “Look at you. You are ” She broke off, searching for a word that could encompass survival, motherhood, dignity, and the quiet strength she read now in her daughter’s eyes. “You are whole.” Regina shook her head, tears still flowing. “Not until now,” she replied. “Not until you.” Behind them, Manuel descended more slowly, leaning on the arm of a younger man whose posture and features marked him as Elias’s kin. His gait was cautious each step measured, as though he knew his body might betray him at any moment but his gaze never left the sight of his wife and daughter embracing. When he reached the bottom of the gangplank, he paused, drawing in a breath that seemed to carry decades of withheld emotion. “Papai,” Regina said, her voice thick, as she turned toward him. He opened his arms not wide, but with a deliberate simplicity that carried more weight than any theatrical gesture and she stepped into them as she had done as a child returning from the marketplace, only now the marketplace was a continent and thirty years long. He smelled of sea salt, old wool, and something else she recognized with a shock: the faint, reassuring scent of ink and parchment. Somehow, through everything, he had remained a man of letters. “My daughter,” he murmured into her hair. “You have your mother’s strength and my stubbornness. It seems Heaven decided that combination was not to be wasted.” She laughed through tears, pressing her face against his shoulder, feeling how frail he had become and yet how solid his embrace remained. A small hand tugged at Regina’s sleeve. Benjamin stood just within reach, his face pale with awe. “Mama,” he whispered, “are these… ?” Regina turned, still holding her father’s hand. “These are your grandparents,” she said, switching instinctively to Portuguese so that the words might wrap themselves around the moment with the intimacy of their shared past. “The ones I told you stories about. They crossed the world to see you.” Raquel’s gaze slid past Regina’s shoulder and fell upon the children. For a heartbeat she simply stared, as if they were apparitions conjured by yearning. Then she moved toward them, her hands trembling. She touched Benjamin’s cheek, Miriam’s hair, little Solomon’s shoulder, as though verifying that they were made of f lesh and not vapor. “You have your grandfather’s eyes,” she whispered to Benjamin. “And your grandmother’s nose,” she added to Miriam, who smiled shyly. To the youngest she said nothing at first, only pressed her lips to his forehead and whispered something too soft to catch. Hanna had hung back, trembling, as if unsure whether she had the right to approach. Her eyes darted between their parents and the ground, her fingers twisting in the fabric of her dress. When Manuel finally saw her clearly, he inhaled sharply, as though struck. “Hanna,” he said, the name cracking in his throat. She looked up, tears already welling. “Papa?” she asked, her voice small and disbelieving. Raquel turned, and for a moment she seemed unable to move. Then something in her broke free. She reached for Hanna with both arms, pulling her close, murmuring her name over and over like a prayer that had finally received an answer. Hanna clung to her, sobbing in great, shaking breaths that shook her whole body, pressing her face into her mother’s shoulder as though seeking to hide from all the lost years between them. “I looked for you in my sleep,” Hanna cried. “I called you, but you did not come. I thought… I thought you were gone.” “I was not gone,” Raquel replied, her own tears falling into her daughter’s hair. “I was wandering like you, in a different darkness. But the same God who led you here has led us to you. We are found now. We are together.” Manuel placed his hand gently on Hanna’s head, his fingers moving in the familiar pattern of blessing. “May the One who protected you when we could not,” he murmured, “now let you rest in the shelter of those who love you.” The dockworkers looked away with a kind of embarrassed respect, pretending not to witness an intimacy they could not fully understand. Elias and his cousin stepped back, allowing the family a small circle of privacy in the midst of the harbor’s noisy bustle. The Brinkmeyer’s, standing a little to one side, watched with faces already wet with tears. When, at last, the embraces loosened enough for words to resume, Regina turned toward her adoptive parents. “Máe, Papai,” she said softly, addressing Manuel and Raquel, “there is something you must know.” She drew the Brinkmeyer’s closer with a gesture. “These are the people who found me in Amsterdam. They gave me work when I had nothing, a bed when I had no home, and their name when my own was too dangerous to speak. They are my parents here, as you are my parents there. Without them, we would not be standing here today.” Raquel looked at Mrs. Brinkmeyer, then at her husband, and in that look passed an entire conversation astonishment, gratitude, a momentary ache that someone else had stood where she had longed to be, followed by the graciousness of a woman too wise to let jealousy stain a blessing. She stepped forward and took Mrs. Brinkmeyer's hands in her own. "You held my child when I could not," she said. "You sheltered her when I could only pray. You wore the name of mother in practice when I could carry it only in memory. I cannot repay you. Only the One above can. But I thank you with all that is left of my strength." Mrs. Brinkmeyer, whose Dutch reserve had often been mistaken for coldness by those who did not know the disciplined heart beating beneath it, allowed her composure to break fully for perhaps the first time in public. "She has been the greatest gift of my life," she replied, her voice thick. "We have waited for this day with her for many years." The two women embraced, Iberian and Dutch, united by the strange fraternity that exists only between mothers who have both lost and regained at least part of what they most loved. The journey from the harbor back to the Toledano house unfolded like a procession, though without music or officialdom. Manuel and Raquel walked slowly, supported by Rafael on one side and Elias's cousin on the other, with the children skipping ahead and running back in excited bursts, torn between curiosity about the city and the need to remain near the grandparents whose presence seemed almost miraculous. Hanna kept close to Raquel's side, one hand clutching the older woman's sleeve, her eyes darting to every sound as if afraid the spell might yet be broken. When they reached the house and stepped inside, Manuel paused in the entryway, closing his eyes for a brief moment. The familiar smell of Sabbath spices seemed to linger in the wood, even though it was not yet Friday. The walls carried the faint echo of children's laughter, of adult voices in quiet conversation, of prayers spoken without fear of eavesdroppers. "This is your home," he said softly to Regina, more statement than question. "Yes," she answered. "Ours. All of ours now, if you will stay." He nodded once, his eyes shining. "We will stay," he said. "If Heaven allows it, we will let our bones rest in this city, and our souls in the presence of your children." Raquel walked to the table where Regina had arranged the relics of her childhood. She reached out and touched each object in turn the silver spoons, the fragment of lace, the small box, the amulet now hanging from a nail above the shelf.

Her fingers trembled, but her expression remained composed, the way a musician's might as she touches the instrument, she once believed lost. "You carried more than I dared hope," she murmured. "These things, and your faith, and your name in your heart." Regina stepped beside her. "I carried what I could," she replied. "The rest I found again here in different forms." The first meal they shared together in the house was not elaborate;

exhaustion and emotion had little appetite for banquet. But its simplicity the crust of bread, the vegetable stew, the small dish of olives and pickled fish, the wine poured into mismatched cups gave it a sacramental quality. Manuel insisted on reciting the blessing over bread, his voice trembling only slightly, then looked up and smiled faintly. "I have spoken these words in hiding, in jail, and over crusts we pretended were loaves," he said. "To say them now in a house where the mezuzah is visible on the doorpost feels like having been given new lungs." That night, long after the children had finally fallen asleep and the candles had burned low, Regina sat alone in the quiet of the front room, listening to the unfamiliar yet profoundly comforting sound of her parents' breathing in the adjacent chamber. She felt a weariness she had never known before, not because of distress, but because of the tension that had sustained her for years the invisible effort of holding together the torn cloth of her identity had, in part, been relieved. She thought of Solomon, of his grave in unseen Portuguese soil, of the brother whose name lived now in her youngest son, whose kindness flowed like an underground river through all of their lives. She accepted, with a strange calm, that not all the dead could be brought across oceans. Some must remain as roots in the old country, feeding, by their hidden presence, the branches that now grew in foreign light. As she finally rose to go to bed, she paused before the shelf of relics. There, beside the amulet and the lace, she placed something new: a small stone she had picked up at the harbor that afternoon, still faintly damp from the sea. It was smooth, unremarkable except for the fact that it existed at the meeting point of water and land, of departure and arrival. It would remain there as a quiet marker of the day when the story had bent toward mercy. For the first time since she had fled Portugal under a false name, she felt that the circle of her life, though not closed, had found at least one of its intended endpoints. Her parents slept under her roof. Her children dreamed in safety. Her sister lay only a few steps away instead of across an unknown distance. The house, once simply a refuge, had become something larger and deeper. It was now a house of returned souls.

CHAPTER 19 THE BRINKMEYER'S FINAL BLESSING

The weeks following the reunion passed with an almost sacred stillness, as if the house were suspended in a fragile pocket of time that knew its peace could not last but wished, for a little while, to pretend otherwise. Manuel and Raquel settled into the home with a grace that astonished even themselves. The Dutch air, colder and more disciplined than the mild breezes of Évora, seemed to steady them rather than burden them. Their tired lungs did not complain of the dampness; their limbs, though stiff, seemed to move more easily now that they no longer feared each knock at the door. Even their sleep, which had been shallow for years, deepened into something approaching rest. It was as if simply being in the same room as their surviving daughters, surrounded by the innocent noise of grandchildren, allowed their bodies to remember their own rhythms. But time, which had granted them this miracle, now began to reveal its price. The Brinkmeyer's, who had long stood as the protective pillars of Regina's life in Amsterdam, were aging as well, and not gently. Mr. Brinkmeyer, whose gentle humming of Portuguese melodies had once filled the house with quiet comfort, now struggled to ascend the stairs without pausing for breath. His hands, once steady enough to measure spices and write in his ledger by candlelight, shook slightly whenever he lifted his cup. Mrs. Brinkmeyer, who had moved with brisk determination through markets and kitchens for decades, now found herself tiring after short walks, her sharp eyes clouded at the edges by something she refused to name out loud. It happened gradually, in the same way that autumn overtakes the late summer without any one leaf announcing the change. It was the small shifts that revealed the truth an unsteady step, a breath drawn too sharply, a cough that lingered after the candles had burned down. Regina noticed before anyone else, not because she was searching for signs, but because she had learned over a lifetime to detect the faintest tremor in the world around her. Life had trained her to recognize fragility where others saw only stillness. One evening, as the family gathered for a modest meal, Manuel offering a blessing with a voice still unexpectedly strong Regina observed that Mrs. Brinkmeyer did not touch her plate. She kept her hands folded in her lap, listening attentively to the conversation but contributing less than usual. Her gaze drifted often to Manuel and Raquel, studying the Spanish couple with a look that mixed admiration with a quiet, almost wistful recognition. When the meal ended and the others dispersed. children chasing candle smoke, Manuel discussing the upcoming Sabbath with Rafael, Hanna carefully gathering plates Regina gently approached her adoptive mother. "You are tired," she said softly. Mrs. Brinkmeyer smiled in the way one smiles when a truth has already been accepted internally but has not yet been granted permission to exist beyond a person's thoughts. "It is nothing," she said. "Age, perhaps. Weariness of the bones. Nothing that time will not cure." Regina knew better. "Time cures nothing," she replied gently. "Time only moves forward. What does not heal grows." The older woman looked at her for a long moment, then placed her hand on Regina's cheek, the way Raquel had done at the harbor. There was a tenderness in that gesture that carried twenty years of unspoken affection the affection of a woman who had helped rebuild another woman's daughter when the world had tried to destroy her. "You have your mother again," she whispered. "And I have lived long enough to see that. It is enough for me." But Regina's eyes filled with tears. "You are my mother too." "Yes," Mrs. Brinkmeyer said, "but not in the way of blood. I knew that the day I found your prayerbook beneath your mattress. I loved you from that moment, but I also accepted that you belonged to someone else. And now those people are here. I feel something inside me loosening, as though my hands, which held you for so long, can finally let go." "I do not want you to let go," Regina said, her voice trembling. "Ah," the older woman murmured, brushing a strand of hair behind Regina's ear, "love always wants to hold on. But wisdom knows when holding on becomes a burden. My dear child, you have a family now more than one. You have children who cling to your skirts, parents who traveled oceans to see you again, a sister who looks to you for guidance, and a husband who knows your soul. My task in this world is nearly finished." Regina felt the words settle into her like a stone dropped into deep water. "What task?" she whispered. "To bring you to where you were meant to be," Mrs. Brinkmeyer said simply. "To carry you across the bridge between who you were and who you have become." In the days that followed, the truth could no longer be ignored. The Brinkmeyer's were fading, each in their own way, each at their own pace, but both unmistakably. The doctor who visited confirmed quietly what Regina had already sensed: there was no illness, no infection, no remedy. Their bodies were simply approaching their appointed time, loosening their grip on the world like leaves preparing to fall. Winter arrived harshly that year, pressing its cold hands against the windows, whitening the canals at dawn, coating the narrow streets with a sheen of frost. Yet inside the Toledano house, the atmosphere was warm, almost liturgical. Regina divided each day between her parents and her adoptive parents, as though she were a bridge between two eras of her own life. Raquel kept vigil for the Brinkmeyer's, bringing them tea, singing softly in Portuguese as she had once sung to her own children. Manuel read aloud from his old prayerbook, his voice steady even when his hands trembled. Rafael repaired a chair in the Brinkmeyer sitting room, fixed a window latch that had grown loose in the cold, sharpened knives, mended cloth anything that might bring comfort. The children, too, played their part, climbing into bed beside Mr. Brinkmeyer to listen to his stories, though his voice sometimes drifted into silence mid-sentence, or singing to Mrs. Brinkmeyer in soft Dutch lullabies that made her smile even when she was too tired to speak. One evening, as the Sabbath approached, Regina lit the candles with her mother and Mrs. Brinkmeyer beside her. It was the first time all three women had stood together at the candlesticks, three versions of motherhood, three keepers of the flame. The candles flickered and elongated, sending long shadows across the table.

Regina covered her eyes, whispering the blessing through tears she did not attempt to hide. When she lowered her hands, she saw both her mothers smiling, the one who had given her life and the one who had given her back her dignity. That night, after the children slept and the house grew quiet, Mr. Brinkmeyer called Regina to his bedside. His breath was shallow and his voice faint, but his eyes were clear. “My child,” he said softly, “there is something I must say before the night carries me too far.” Regina sat beside him and took his hand, which felt light as parchment. He looked at her with a tenderness so profound that she felt the years fold back, revealing not the frail elder lying in the bed but the man who had once welcomed a frightened, penniless Portuguese girl into his home without hesitation. “You gave my life meaning,” he whispered. “Not through service or obligation, but through your courage. When you came to us alone, trembling, carrying only your name and your faith, you brought into our home a light we had not known we were missing. You made us more than merchants. You made us parents.” Regina tried to speak, but her throat was constricted. “You will carry our name in your heart,” he continued, “even when you no longer carry it on paper. That is enough. And now, before I go, I ask you only this: teach your children the same kindness you showed us. If they walk through the world with even half your compassion, they will carry our blessing without needing our blood.” He closed his eyes, exhausted by the effort, but squeezed her hand once more. “I bless you,” he murmured. “In the name of all that is good, I bless you.” He slept then, deeply, and Regina remained by his side until dawn. He passed quietly the next morning, his hand still in hers, as if he simply drifted from one dream into another. When she closed his eyes, she did so with a reverence that felt ancient, older than Amsterdam, older than Portugal, older even than the exile that had shaped her life. Mrs. Brinkmeyer followed only a day later. She had sat upright earlier in the day, her back supported by pillows, her eyes bright with a strange vigor that Regina immediately recognized not the stirring of health, but the gathering of the last reserves of strength before the final letting go. “Do not weep for me,” she told Regina, pressing a hand against her cheek. "I have lived enough for several lifetimes. I have been mother to a child I did not bear, and grandmother to children who carry only the imprint of my love. I leave nothing unfinished." When her breath grew thin and her eyes clouded, Regina sat beside her, holding her hand in the same way she had held her fathers long ago. Raquel held her other hand. Hanna stood at the foot of the bed, trembling but determined not to flee. In her final moments, Mrs. Brinkmeyer whispered something hoarse but clear. "You were the greatest joy of my life." And then she was gone. The funerals were held with solemn dignity. The entire Portuguese Jewish community attended, walking behind the simple coffins with heads bowed in respect for the graceful, compassionate couple who had sheltered one of their own in the darkest of times. Rabbi Aron delivered a eulogy so tender that even the children remained silent, sensing the weight of what was being spoken. Manuel recited a prayer in Portuguese, Rafael in Hebrew, and Regina in Dutch. The three languages mingled like the intertwined roots of the life she had built complex, layered, inseparable. When the earth covered the coffins and the kaddish was said, by Rafael, Regina remained standing beside the graves long after the others had departed. The winter wind tugged at her shawl, but she did not shiver. Her grief was not the old, sharp grief that had followed her from Portugal; it was deep but gentle, like the weight of a well-made blanket. She knelt and placed three stones upon each grave. One stone for gratitude. One stone for love. One stone for the years they had carried her. As she rose, she felt two familiar hands slip into hers one warm and weathered, the other thin and trembling. Raquel and Manuel stood beside her, their faces solemn yet peaceful. "They blessed you with everything they had," Manuel said softly. "Now you will carry that blessing forward." "Yes," Regina whispered, squeezing their hands. "I will." Together they walked back toward the house, where the children waited and the Sabbath candles would soon be lit again. A house that had once been a refuge had now become a sanctuary of generations past, present, and future. A house that carried grief and love in equal measures. A house where two sets of parents had blessed the same daughter. A house of light.

CHAPTER 20 A LEGACY REBORN

Amsterdam, 1658 The house on the Bloemgracht, once merely a refuge for a frightened girl with borrowed names and trembling hands, had by now grown into something far larger than even Regina could have imagined. Its beams had absorbed decades of sighs and prayers, music and grief, children's laughter and whispered blessings. The air within its walls held the faint scent of cinnamon and cloves, unchanged from the days when Mrs. Brinkmeyer arranged her jars with meticulous pride, and yet there was a deeper fragrance now the warmth of a home shaped by a woman who had rebuilt herself piece by piece, flame by flame, until memory and hope lived side by side like the tall candles she lit each Friday night. Regina moved more slowly these days, though her mind remained sharp and her voice steady. Her hair, once dark, had softened into silver threads that framed her face like the delicate lace caps of Dutch matrons. Her hands still moved with certainty her mother's hands, her grandmother's hands and when she held a book or traced a Hebrew line in her prayer-pages, there was a quiet authority in her gestures, as though she were touching not ink but the very continuation of her people. The community around her had changed as well. What began as a small, hidden group of Iberian Jews gathering in attics and back rooms had blossomed into a confident, learned congregation. Synagogues rose with careful dignity; merchants and scholars from across the Atlantic and the Mediterranean found their place among the Dutch; ships carried letters and goods across oceans; refugees arrived weekly from Spain, Portugal, Livorno, Brazil, Morocco, even the far islands of the Caribbean. Amsterdam had become a harbor not only of trade but of souls, and Regina's home had become one of its quiet centers of gravity. It was Rafael who had insisted, years ago, that they keep the Brinkmeyer household open to those who arrived with little more than fear and a foreign tongue. "We were strangers," he reminded her gently, "and it was a stranger who gave you bread." And so the tradition began: a room kept ready, a meal offered without question, a space made for the lost to rest their feet until they remembered the shape of their own names again. Some stayed for days, some for months, and a rare few remained for years, weaving themselves into the fabric of the household until they moved forward with renewed dignity. Their children had long since grown into adults whose identities seemed to rest smoothly upon the dual axes that had shaped them: Portuguese in soul, Dutch in discipline; Jews in pride, citizens of the world in vision. Their eldest son, Elias named after the traveler who had brought news of their parents was now a merchant whose ships crossed from Recife to Antwerp and back, carrying sugar, spices, and texts in Hebrew and Portuguese. Their daughter Miriam, gentle yet unyieldingly precise, taught reading and writing to children from families who had lived for generations under the shadow of the Inquisition. Their youngest, Samuel, walked with the air of a scholar, his fingers always stained with ink, his mind perpetually dancing between the Torah of his ancestors and the philosophy of Amsterdam's emerging intellectual circles. Regina watched them with a quiet awe she never tired of feeling. Each carried a fragment of the past within them, but none were burdened by it; they walked freely, as though the centuries of silence and fear had finally loosened their grip. Sometimes, on quiet afternoons, one could find Regina seated in the attic that had once been her maid's chamber, though it had long since been transformed into a study filled with books from across the Jewish world. She would sit beside the small window overlooking the canal and trace the margins of her mother's old prayerbook the very one that had nearly cost her safety in her youth. Its pages were fragile now, its Portuguese notes faded, but she handled it as though it were a living relative, a voice whispering across decades: Do not forget who you are, and do not forget who walked before you. One afternoon, as she held this book open upon her lap, she heard footsteps on the stairs light, urgent, unmistakably young. Her granddaughter, Sarit, burst into the room with the unrestrained enthusiasm of childhood. "Avoó," she exclaimed, breathless, "Mama says there is someone downstairs you must meet." Regina smiled at the girl's excitement. "Is it one of your mother's pupils?" "No," the girl said, shaking her head, curls bouncing. "Someone new. Someone who speaks like you, with the Portuguese sounds." Regina's breath caught for an instant a habit she had never fully unlearned, but she closed the prayerbook carefully and followed Sarit downstairs. In the main room stood a young woman, thin, trembling, clutching a small cloth bag to her chest. Her face held the unmistakable marks of flight: exhaustion etched into the lines of her mouth, fear lingering beneath her eyes, the posture of someone who has not slept properly in months. Yet when her gaze lifted and met Regina's, a wave of recognition passed between them not of individual memory, but of shared history, shared suffering, shared survival. Rafael stepped forward. "She arrived on the morning ship from Hamburg," he explained softly. "Her family f led Lisbon last year. She has been searching for our community since she reached the city." The young woman swallowed, her voice fragile but determined. "They told me... they told me that here... there would be a house where a woman who understands would receive me." Regina approached her slowly, not as a matron, not as a hostess, but as a mirror of what she herself had once been. The young refugee held out a folded letter with shaking hands. Regina accepted it gently, her fingers brushing the girl's for a moment that conveyed more comfort than words ever could. "Here," Regina said, her voice warm, strong, steady, "no one remains a stranger." The girl burst into tears the sudden, uncontrollable kind that come only after too many nights of forced silence. Regina drew her close, holding her the way her own mother had held her in that long-awaited reunion not so many years ago. And as she embraced the trembling newcomer, Regina felt something settled within her a realization, vast and quiet, that the suffering she had endured had not ended with her; it had transformed her into a vessel through which others could find healing. In the months that followed, the girl whose name was Beatriz became part of the household much as Regina once had. She learned to grind cinnamon, to recite blessings openly, to write her name not in fear but in pride. Regina taught her melodies from Portugal, and the girl taught Regina new ones carried from the hills of Alentejo. The house, always filled with echoes, now carried the music of yet another voice. As Regina's strength declined, the community did not see her as a fading presence but as a burning one a torch passed carefully from hand to hand. Rabbis sought her counsel; young mothers sought her blessings; merchants consulted her when disputes arose; and refugees carried her name across oceans as a symbol of the kindness waiting for them in Amsterdam. When she finally reached her final days, she asked to be carried to the same attic room where her new life had begun. The window overlooked the canal as it always had, and the scent of spices drifted faintly upward from the kitchen. Rafael sat beside her, their children gathered quietly near the stairs, their grandchildren huddled close, whispering questions they did not fully understand. Regina held her mother's prayerbook one last time. She touched its cover with reverence, then handed it to Miriam. "Guard this," she said, her voice soft but unwavering. "It belongs to all of us now." As dusk fell and the shadows of the rooftops lengthened across the water, Regina whispered the same words she had spoken as a girl beneath her hidden Shabbat candle a blessing for light in dark places. Her eyes closed slowly, peacefully, not with the weariness of a life scarred by exile, but with the serenity of a life completed. In the years that followed, the household remained a sanctuary.

Refugees continued to arrive; children continued to grow; Shabbat candles continued to shine across the canal like small, determined stars. And every Friday evening, as the flames were kindled and blessings whispered, those who gathered around the Brinkmeyer table felt a presence woven into the very walls the steady, enduring spirit of Regina Nunez Vas, the girl who fled Portugal and became the mother of a people reborn.

EPILOGUE THE CANDLES OF THE NÚÑEZ VÁS HOUSE

The Bloemgracht lay quiet beneath a sky washed in winter blue, the kind of pale, translucent light that seemed to hold memory the way water holds reflections. Thin sheets of frost clung to the canal's wooden edges, and the wind carried the faint scent of smoke from distant chimneys. It was the final hour before dusk, that brief, delicate threshold where day yields to night without protest, and night accepts its mantle with slow, solemn dignity. Inside the old Brinkmeyer house, the one that had belonged to merchants, then to wanderers, then to an entire lineage of reborn souls, the air was thick with the warmth of gathering. Grandchildren and great grandchildren whispered excitedly; daughters and sons moved through the rooms with the calm familiarity of those who had grown up under the shelter of its beams; neighbors from the community merchants, scholars, widows, sailors, teachers, refugees drifted in with reverent steps, each aware that tonight was not simply another Shabbat, but the anniversary of the night Regina Núñez Vás had first lit her hidden candle as a free woman in Amsterdam. They gathered because the house had asked for it. Or perhaps because the memory of Regina had asked for it. Some said they felt her presence most vividly on winter evenings, others in the whisper of the spice jars when the kitchen door was opened, still others in the attic where her mother's prayerbook rested beneath glass. But all of them agreed that her spirit lingered not as a ghost, but as a light a steady flame, quiet and unwavering. Hanna, older now but still sharp-eyed and steady, stood near the window where she had once helped Regina grind cinnamon. Her hair, long since silver, was wrapped in a kerchief embroidered with tiny Portuguese roses. She watched the grandchildren move about the room children who bore neither Portugal's scars nor its fear, only its melodies and memories and she felt the bittersweet ache of gratitude that age brings. Samuel, Rafael and Regina's youngest, now an elder in his own right, approached her with a gentle smile. "You should sit," he murmured. "You've been standing too long." "I stood beside your mother for fifty years," Hanna replied, her voice firm but softened by affection. "I can stand a little longer in her house." Samuel nodded. He understood. All of them did. No one argued with Hanna on the anniversary of Regina's first Shabbat in freedom. The room gradually settled. Conversations faded into a murmuring hush. The children were gathered near the long wooden table, now covered in embroidered cloth passed down from Regina's mother the same cloth that had once traveled tucked in a trunk from Lisbon to Amsterdam, crossing borders like a quiet witness to history. At the head of the table stood Sarit, Regina's granddaughter, now a woman with gentle hands and a voice that carried like warm honey. Tonight, she would light the candles. It had been her role since the passing of Regina, not because she was the eldest, but because she had been the one who loved most fiercely to listen to Regina's stories. She placed two tall candles into silver holders, the very candlesticks the Brinkmeyer's had once gifted Regina when she married Rafael. Their bases were engraved with tiny ships, spices, and vines symbols of the worlds that had intertwined to make this home. The windows dimmed as dusk edged forward. The canal outside darkened into a slate mirror. Inside, the air grew expectant, like the held breath before a song begins. Sarit raised her hands. The room stilled. And then she lit the first flame. The wick caught with a soft trembling glow, expanding in steady circles until the room warmed in its radius. The second candle followed a twin flame rising with gentle confidence. The two lights leaned toward one another as though greeting like old friends, sending golden ribbons across the tablecloth. Sarit closed her eyes and whispered the blessing the blessing that had once been whispered by Regina under her bed in Portugal, whispered again in terror behind a locked attic door, whispered in hope on her first free Shabbat in

Amsterdam, whispered through decades of exile transformed into home. When Sarit finished, she remained still for a moment, her hands covering her eyes, letting the silence settle the way Regina had taught her: not as absence, but as presence. Then she lowered her hands. And every person in the room felt it a shift, gentle but undeniable, as if the air itself welcomed someone ancient and beloved. It was Hanna who spoke first, her voice soft. “She is here.” Sarit nodded. “She is always here.” The candles flickered, casting their light across the faces of those gathered. Young eyes reflected golden halos; older eyes reflected decades of memory. Some of the elders whispered prayers; others simply watched the f lames with a reverence born not of ritual alone, but of recognition that the light before them had been carried through fire, sea, exile, betrayal, courage, and faith. Samuel stepped forward to open the old prayerbook Regina’s, with its worn leather cover and fading Portuguese notes. The pages released a faint scent of age and salt and oil, as if the centuries themselves had exhaled. He recited a chapter of Psalms in a voice that trembled not from frailty but from emotion. When he finished, he looked up at the gathered family and community. “My mother believed that light was not only something we lit,” he said gently. “She believed it was something we carried. Each of you is here because she gave you a f lame whether through her kindness, her guidance, her courage, or the home she built from the ashes of fear.” He closed the prayerbook reverently. “And now it is our turn to carry it forward.” The murmured “amen” rose like a single breath, unified and full. Outside, the canal reflected the candlelight through the windows, scattering their glow into the water where it shimmered like broken stars drifting in slow circles. Boats passed softly, their lanterns dipping in gentle rhythm. The world outside continued, unaware of the sacred memory unfolding behind the tall, narrow walls. Inside, Sarit began to sing the old melody the soft, winding Portuguese tune Regina had taught her. Others joined. The harmony swelled, warm and haunting, weaving past and present into a single song. Hanna closed her eyes and smiled, hearing not only the voices of the living, but the echoes of all those who had come before Regina's mother Miriam, her father Abraham, her brother Solomon whose soul had given birth to courage in others, the Brinkmeyer's who had offered shelter without knowing they were shaping a future generation, and countless unnamed ancestors who had carried the same fragile flame across continents. When the song ended, the room remained quiet, united not by silence but by fullness. The candles burned steadily, unshaken by the drafts that wandered through the old house. Their flames stretched upward, slender and bright, like two unwavering pillars. And then, as the final light of dusk faded beyond the canal and the stars began to prick the darkening sky, Sarit whispered the words that had once belonged to Regina alone, but now belonged to an entire lineage: "May these candles guard our home. May their light guide all who wander. And may their flame never die." The family breathed as one. The candles shone. And the legacy of the Núñez Vás house built on exile, rebuilt on faith, sustained by kindness continued, as eternal as the flame that first began in a hidden attic room beneath a young woman's trembling hands.

Shalom for all folks from different strokes.

About the Author — D. Nunez Vas

D. Nunez Vas is the literary pen name of Rabbi Dovied Zwi van der Velde, a writer whose soul carries centuries of Jewish memory.

This pen name is not an invention—it is an homage. It honors his Sephardic ancestors, the Nunez Vas family of Portugal and Spain, who walked out of fire and exile in the early 1600s so their children could live openly as Jews in the daylight of Amsterdam. They abandoned fortune, comfort, and social standing, choosing instead the privilege—and the cost—of serving God without disguise. Their courage is the living heartbeat of this novel.

Born in Holland, Rabbi van der Velde stands at the crossroads of two heroic lineages: Sephardic perseverance and Ashkenazi resistance.

A Legacy of Quiet Heroism

On his mother's side, Sylvia van der Velde–Duis (Tzila bas Dovied), זכר צדיק לברכה, descended from Dutch Jews whose compassion and bravery shaped entire generations. Her father, David Duis, helped Jews escape Germany during the dangerous years between the two World Wars—quietly, humbly, without recognition, guided only by conscience and love for his people.

Her stepfather, Sal Joseph Witteboon, became one of the author's most formative influences. A withdrawn man, deeply scarred by what he witnessed during the Nazi era, he was active in the Dutch underground. By bicycle, he transported Jewish infants to hiding places, risking execution with every mile he traveled.

Though outwardly distant from religious life, his faith lived deep within him. As a young boy, the author once brought his tefillin into his home, fearful they might be damaged. Instead, the old man carefully unwrapped them, held the shel yad and shel rosh separately, kissed each one, wrapped them again with reverence, kissed the bag, and returned them silently. In that moment, the author understood: this was a man who believed deeply in Hashem—but who had been too wounded by what he had seen to return outwardly.

Survival Against Erasure

From his father's side comes a saga of exile, survival, and divine providence.

His father, Benno (Benyamin Zev ben Dovied Zwi [Hartog]) van der Velde, ה׳ יִנְקוֹם דָּמוֹ, was born in the Dutch East Indies in 1933, where his parents had moved for Jewish communal work. During the Second World War, the family was imprisoned under Japanese occupation. On the first day of Rosh Hashanah, the author's grandfather was killed when the prisoner transport ship on which he was held was torpedoed at sea. May his blood be avenged.

His grandmother, זֵכֶר צַדִּיקָה לִבְרָכָה, survived the hell of Japanese concentration camps—places whose cruelty many survivors said rivaled, and sometimes surpassed, Nazi camps. Under threat of death and despite daily beatings, she secretly taught Jewish children alef-bet, prayer, and faith, and she buried those who died with dignity. She survived as an agunah for thirty-six years after the war.

The author remembers her vividly: the scent of her home, the early-morning exercises she made him do, the sweet eggs she prepared when he stayed overnight, the plastic covering over her drinking glass so the water would not remain uncovered at night. She often told him, in Dutch and Yiddish:

"Daviedje, vergeet nooit de vijfde boek van de Shulchan Aruch."
"Don't forget the fifth volume of the Shulchan Aruch."

When he answered that there were only four volumes, she would smile and reply:

“Those are the written ones. The fifth is how to be a mensch. Remember—your grandfather is watching you from above.”

He remembers the night she returned her soul to Hashem. He was about thirteen. She whispered his father’s name, asked him to say Shema, and said quietly: “Ik ga terug. Je vader wacht op me.” “I’m going back. Your father is waiting for me.”His father and aunt survived the war as young children and were placed with non-Jewish families in Switzerland before eventually being reunited with their mother. Despite illness caused by years of malnutrition and imprisonment, his father went on to study engineering and economics, build a family, and become the author’s greatest hero and example.

Together with his mother, Sylvia (Tzila bas Dovied), זכר צדיק לברכה, the authors sister, and him self. they built a home rich in faith, resilience, and love—raising children and grandchildren who today number in the dozens of souls, kein yirbu.

The author’s aunt, also a survivor, later moved to Israel, where she and her husband built a life of Torah and quiet devotion. From them emerged generations numbering in the hundreds—a living refutation of those who sought Jewish extinction.

The Author Today:

Rabbi van der Velde has devoted his life to community leadership, teaching, and writing. He

triumphs of his own life.

From the Ashes of Lisbon is his tribute to all who lived al Kiddush Hashem: to those who hid their faith behind locked doors, to those who resisted tyranny, and to the families who surrendered wealth and safety so their descendants could serve God freely.

This novel is more than a story.

It is a remembrance, a prayer, and a bridge of light between past and future.

It honors ancestors whose courage became inheritance—and stands as a testament to a Jewish soul that refuses to die, refuses to forget, and refuses to stop shining.

If you wish to know the author more deeply, each of his books reveals a different facet of his inner world.

So—you know what to do.

www.ingramcontent.com/pod-product-compliance
Lightning Source LLC
Chambersburg PA
CBHW081134300726
48982CB00005B/970
* 9 7 9 8 9 9 9 7 6 5 0 4 8 *